Changeling Press, LLC

ChangelingPress.com

Venom/Torch Duet

Harley Wylde

Venom/Torch Duet
Harley Wylde

ISBN: 9781717986856

Publisher:
Changeling Press LLC
315 N. Centre St.
Martinsburg, WV 25404
ChangelingPress.com

Printed in the U.S.A.

Editor: Crystal Esau
Cover Artist: Bryan Keller

The individual stories in this anthology have been previously released in E-Book format.

Table of Contents

Venom (Dixie Reapers MC 1)

Harley Wylde

Ridley: I might live in a mansion in South Florida, but my daddy was a biker, and I was definitely Daddy's girl. When I found out my mom and stepdad had something horrible planned for me, I ran. Straight to the Dixie Reapers, the only place I'd ever thought of as home, but it wasn't my daddy's arms I ended up in. Venom is dark and seductive, the type of man who doesn't take shit from anyone. Despite his hard exterior, being with him makes me feel safe, and his kisses make me ache for so much more. I've never been with a man before, but even as inexperienced as I am, I know that being with Venom will ruin me for anyone else, and I don't care. I want him -- all of him -- and damn the consequences.

Venom: I hadn't risen to the rank of VP of the Dixie Reapers MC without getting my hands dirty. I'd been deep in blood and dirty money for over twenty years, could have any pussy I wanted whenever I wanted and how the fuck ever I wanted. But when an angel I hadn't seen in fourteen years came back into my life, all it took was one look in her eyes, and I was a goner. As a kid, Ridley had been this little blonde cherub who lit up the place. Now she's older, has curves in all the right fucking places, and damn if I don't want her. The fact she was the nineteen-year-old daughter of a patched member meant I needed to keep my hands to myself, and I might have, if she hadn't begged me so sweetly. Now she's mine, and I'll do anything to keep her safe, even if it means starting a war.

Prologue

Fourteen Years Ago
Venom

The little girl with the blonde curls had to be the most beautiful thing I'd ever seen. Her angelic smile could even warm my cold-ass heart. It was still a mystery to me how someone like Bull could have created a kid like that. Hell, I couldn't even imagine a woman pretty enough to make that child even existing. She was like a little china doll and had wrapped every one of my MC brothers around her little finger. Me included.

At the age of twenty-five, I'd never thought about having kids. Honestly, just the thought of knocking up one of the club sluts was enough to keep my dick from getting hard. Easy pussy could be had anytime I wanted it, but accepting my brothers' sloppy seconds, thirds, or tenths, hadn't appealed to me since my days as a Prospect. Oh, I got my dick wet, but I was a little more discerning about where I stuck it.

The gorgeous angel, all of five years old, turned that winning smile my way, and I felt myself melt. Yeah, she was going to be a heartbreaker when she got bigger, that was for damn sure. And she'd have an entire MC ready to go to battle for her. Bull almost seemed sad when he looked at his daughter, and I couldn't figure out why. The child's mom was a raging bitch, but last I'd heard, the courts had granted Bull every other weekend with the girl. We'd had a family day at the clubhouse every Saturday that Bull had his daughter, just so she could hang out with everyone. Which meant no club sluts allowed.

When her mom came to pick her up, Bull seemed to hug the girl a little tighter than usual. The blonde angel waved and smiled at everyone as her mother practically dragged her out of the clubhouse. The old ladies in the corner gave a disapproving stare, but they kept their mouths shut. No one wanted to cause problems for Bull, not when he'd fought so hard to get to see his child at all. Judges didn't look too kindly on outlaws, and Bull had spent some time behind bars, more than once.

Bull lumbered over and sat heavily on the barstool next to me. Waving to a Prospect behind the counter, he ordered a bottle of Jack, looking like the weight of the world was on his shoulders.

"What the fuck, man?" I asked. "You just got to see that gorgeous girl of yours."

"It's bad, man," Bull said. "I've loved that little girl since the moment she was born. Other than the MC, she's the only bright spot I've got."

"And you'll see her again in a few weeks."

Bull shook his head. "This was my last visit with Ridley."

"What the fuck?"

"Her mom's getting remarried. Found some rich guy in South Florida. Guy has a fucking mansion and a yacht. They're moving tomorrow. I have permission to fly down there and see her twice a year for a week each stay, but because of her age, the courts agreed that it would be best if Ridley didn't travel here unless her mom was with her. And we know that's never going to happen."

I let his words sink in, and I glanced at the door where Ridley had disappeared just moments before. It didn't seem right, separating a kid from her dad. I firmed my jaw and stared at him.

"So that's it? You're giving up?" I asked.

"What am I supposed to do?"

"Get your ass to Florida twice a year to see your kid." *Dumbass.*

Bull sighed. "Yeah. I can do that, but she's growing up so damn fast. What if she forgets about me? Her new stepdaddy is all kinds of rich and can give her everything I can't. What if she doesn't want me anymore? I'm just some broke-ass biker who drinks and swears too fucking much."

"Man, I don't care how loaded the guy is. You're always going to be her Pop. That little girl loves the shit out of you, and she always will. Ridley's too smart to let money fuck up her life. She might be five, but she's smarter than most kids her age. Hell, she's probably smarter than her bitch-ass mother."

"Yeah." Bull laughed. "You might be right about that. She's certainly smarter than me. Man, I don't know how I got so lucky to have such a perfect little girl. You're right, though. I'm going to see her every time I'm allowed, and I will call her every fucking day to tell her how much I love her."

I clapped Bull on the back and stood up. "One day Ridley will be all grown up and will be able to make her own decisions. Until then, you do what you can to make sure she knows she'll always be your number one girl."

"Thanks, Venom. You're a good kid."

I snorted. Kid. Hell, Bull was only ten years older than me. Grabbing my keys out of my pocket, I strolled out to my bike. I could feel the energy pulsing inside me and knew I needed a wild ride to calm me down. And if that didn't work, then I'd find a willing woman and work it off that way. My favorite bar on the other side of town was calling my name. The liquor flowed like honey, and the women were fine as hell. And I planned to enjoy both tonight.

Chapter One

I'd been looking forward to my nineteenth birthday for the past year. Nothing overly special about that number, but it meant I was finally free of this hell. I'd been convinced to stick around one more year when I'd turned eighteen, even though I'd had every intention of running straight to my daddy. But after what my mother said, I wasn't sure my dad would want me, and I had nowhere else to go. She'd talked me out of college, and against my better judgment, I'd let her. I don't know why. Maybe it was some misguided feeling that maybe, just maybe, she really loved me and everything would work out.

My mother had married Richard Benton III, a man more than twice her age, when I was five years old. He'd never had kids, and at first had treated me well. Then Mom had gotten pregnant when I was nine, and an heir had been born. I couldn't blame the kid for my problems, not really. He was innocent in all this. Well, mostly. At the age of ten, he was already something of a snot, but I knew it was because his daddy gave him everything he ever wanted.

Mom had knocked on my door an hour ago and told me to shower and put on the dress she'd hung on the back of my closet door. I'd argued, reminding her I had plans with my friends, but she'd waved me off and said this was more important. Little did she realize those plans were actually a large backpack full of clothes hidden in my car, along with a pair of boots, and a full tank of gas. I'd planned to hit the road and go home where I belonged, with the Dixie Reapers MC. But it seemed Richard had someone coming to dinner, and we would be spending the night at home as a family. I was fuming mad, but experience taught me it was better to do as they said. If Dad knew half the shit my mom had put me through, he'd have broken her damn neck, and sometimes I thought about telling him. All I had to do was get through dinner, then I could get the hell out of this place for the last time. I hadn't told Dad I was coming, but I hoped he'd welcome me. I knew Mom had turned him away when he'd last visited, and he was probably angry, maybe even angrier that I hadn't reached out since then. But I was his little girl, and I was hoping that still meant something to him. Even if I had screwed up.

I was showered, shaved, and dressed in the cocktail dress Mom had left, which molded to my curves and was a little shorter than I liked. My makeup was done to perfection, and my hair was curling down my back. I had to admit I looked good, and more grown-up than ever before. Stepping into my kitten heels, I heard the doorbell ring and made my way downstairs. If I made them wait, I would be punished. Not in front of guests, of course. They'd wait until their company left, and then all hell would break loose. And I couldn't afford to let that happen if I planned to escape tonight. I had planned everything as best I could, without drawing too much attention to myself, even going so far as to purchase clothes more suited to life in an MC than the mansion that horrified me. I couldn't go overboard, though, because Mom and the stepass watched my account activity, since they were the ones putting money into it in the first place.

A man in an impeccable suit stood in the foyer, his hair, more salt than pepper, was slicked back and shone under the lights. The smile plastered on his face was oily, the type you'd find on politicians and used car salesmen. But the coldness of his dark gaze made me wish I'd defied Mom after all. He studied me as I descended the staircase, his gaze caressing every inch of my body as if he were undressing me. A chill skated down my spine, and my steps faltered.

My stepdad smiled brightly when he saw me. "Ridley, come meet our guest. This is Fernando Montoya. A business associate of mine."

I made my way down the rest of the steps and stopped beside my mother and stepdad. I looked at Mr. Montoya and couldn't help but think something was very wrong. For one, where was my little brother? If this was a family dinner, shouldn't he have been invited too? For another, I'd seen men like this one before. Even my father, who was as badass as they came, didn't have the cold stare this man did, and I had no doubt there was blood on my dad's hands. For the first time in my life, I knew true fear. I didn't yet understand what was going on, but I didn't like it.

"You're being rude to our guest, Ridley. Say hello."

"Hello, Mr. Montoya."

"Ridley." His smile chilled me.

"Well," my mother said brightly. "I believe dinner is ready. Shall we go to the dining room? Cook has prepared lobster bisque, crab cakes, shrimp scampi, and almond encrusted tilapia. And she has something very special planned for dessert."

The smirk on my stepdad's face was another clue that something wasn't right. Somehow, I had to get myself out of this situation, and I needed to do it fast. Every alarm in my body was screaming for me to bolt and not to stop running until I reached the Dixie Reapers compound. My mom and stepdad might have money, but even they wouldn't darken that doorstep.

Not uninvited anyway, and no way in hell were they ever getting that invitation. Dad had made it no secret that if Mom and Richard were to suddenly drop dead, he'd dance at the funeral and piss on their graves. Especially after his last arrest. Mom had made sure all his visitation rights were revoked, and I hadn't seen my old man in over two years. We'd still talked... at first, but it wasn't the same.

He came to the house when I turned eighteen, but I hadn't been allowed to see him. He'd kicked up a fuss until the police came to escort him away. What had hurt the most was Mom telling him that I didn't want anything to do with a dirty biker like him. I hoped like hell he hadn't believed her. The phone calls from him had stopped right after that, and I hadn't had the courage to pick up the phone and call.

We trailed after her. I took the seat beside her, like I always did, and Mr. Montoya sat on Richard's other side. But the looks he kept casting my way made me uneasy. Mom noticed the attention the older man was giving me and gave another one of those falsely bright smiles.

"Ridley, why don't you go sit next to Mr. Montoya. I'm sure he'd love the company after such a long journey."

I tried to hide the fact I was quaking in my fashionable heels as I stood and moved around the table. Mr. Montoya stood and pulled out my chair. As he pushed it back under the table after I'd sat, his hands caressed my bare shoulders. Revulsion rolled through me, and I felt like I'd been touched by Death himself. He reclaimed his seat and began a conversation with my stepdad, but all throughout the meal, his hand wandered to inappropriate places under the table. When he shoved his hand up my dress, shoved my panties aside and stroked my pussy, I bolted out of my chair so fast it tipped over.

"S-sorry," I stammered. "Bathroom."

Without waiting to be excused, I ran from the room. My heart thundered in my chest as I locked myself in the bathroom off the foyer. The air duct over my head had always carried sounds from the dining room, and I listened in horror as my stepdad and Mr. Montoya discussed me like I was cattle.

"She'll do," Mr. Montoya said. "I'll have fun breaking her in. Once she's been properly trained, I'm sure she'll fetch top dollar."

My stomach pitched, and I nearly threw up.

"Of course, I'd prefer to see all the merchandise before paying our agreed upon price," Mr. Montoya said. "After dinner, I'll see exactly what I'm paying for and maybe take her for a test drive."

"Whatever you need," my mom said. "This deal is very important to us."

Holy shit! My own mother was selling me? Shit like this just didn't happen. Not to girls like me. Yeah, sure, you heard on the news about women being sold overseas to brothels, but to have it brought to own my front door... My hand shook as I slowly turned the knob and let myself out of the bathroom. I removed my heels so I wouldn't make a sound.

Marta, the housekeeper we'd had since I first moved here, was quietly standing near the front door. Out of sight of the dining room. With a quick glance toward the door that led to where my fate awaited, I dashed to Marta's side. She handed me my purse and car keys.

"Be safe," she whispered. "Go straight to your father."

"Marta, I..."

She shushed me and gave me a tight hug. "I love you like you were my own. I won't stand by and let this happen to you. Now go, before they realize you're not coming back."

"Thank you," I said fervently, then soundlessly opened the front door and made my escape.

My car, a Mercedes Richard and Mom had bought on my sixteenth birthday, was parked around the side of the house. The engine was quiet, and if I kept my headlights off, no one would even know I was leaving. I slipped behind the wheel and tossed my purse and shoes on the passenger seat. Fastening my seatbelt, I shut the door as softly as I could and started the engine.

The car crept around the fountain and down the driveway. The gate remained open from when Mr. Montoya had arrived, and I breathed a sigh of relief. Once my tires touched the road, I flicked on my headlights and headed for the highway. It was a long-ass drive to Alabama, but except for gas, I wasn't fucking stopping until I saw my daddy. Mom might have done her best to separate us, but I would always be Daddy's little girl.

When I'd been on the road for hours, my stomach began to cramp from hunger and my car was almost on empty. I pulled into a small town somewhere in North Florida. After filling my tank, I left the car parked at the gas station and walked across the street to a diner. But what I saw when I stepped through the doors froze me in my tracks. My face was plastered across the TV with a ticker running underneath. *Ridley Johnson is reported as being unstable. If seen, contact the police immediately.*

I tried to pull my hair forward as much as possible to hide my face and claimed a spot at the back of the diner, where the lighting wasn't so great. My hands fumbled with my purse, and I quietly counted what was left of my cash. I'd seen enough crime shows to know my credit cards could be traced, so I'd paid cash at the gas station and I'd pay cash for my meal. An older waitress came over, looking dead on her feet.

"What can I get you, doll?"

"A burger and fries with a sweet tea."

She nodded and scribbled my order down, not even looking at my face once. As she moved away to place my order with the kitchen, some of the tension eased from my shoulders. The place was nearly empty, but I had a close call when a sheriff's deputy stepped inside. I sat frozen, scared to even breathe, until he picked up his to-go order and went back out to his cruiser.

My meal arrived a few minutes later, and I ate quickly, leaving enough money on the table to cover the bill and a tip. Gathering my purse, I headed back to my car, every nerve in my body on alert for any kind of trouble. I hit the road again and didn't stop until I'd cleared the panhandle. The town was shabby, the sidewalks cracked, and the buildings crumbling. I stuck out like a sore thumb, but it was time to change. I stopped to top off my tank at a gas station that was well lit, just in case I got stuck with the car a while longer, and grabbed my backpack from the trunk. In case my family had gotten nosy, I'd hidden it in the spare tire compartment, which meant if I had a flat I was shit out of luck because both the tire and my bag and boots hadn't fit.

After filling up the car, I stepped into the grimy bathroom and stripped out of my dress and heels. I washed my face in the sink with the harsh soap provided in the dispenser and blotted it dry with the stiffest damn paper towels I'd ever touched. Pulling an elastic from my bag, I pulled my hair up into a ponytail, the long curling mass falling down the center of my back. After I had shimmied into a pair of tight, ripped jeans and put on a black tee with teal swirls and white skulls across the front, I slipped on some socks and the biker boots I'd picked up at a Harley Davidson store.

A smile flashed across my face as I studied my reflection in the cracked mirror. Aside from the golden curls, I didn't even look like Ridley Johnson anymore. At least, not the Ridley Johnson Mom had molded me to be. I hated that girl and never wanted to be her again. I stuffed my dress and heels in the trash, picked up my bag, and went back out to my car. The guy behind the counter didn't even look up from his magazine.

Now I just had one more problem. The damn car. There was no way my stepdad had put out that bulletin on me without also telling the cops what I was driving. It was a fucking miracle no one had pulled me over yet. I knew what I was about to do was risky as hell, but so was driving around in this damn Mercedes for another minute.

I'd hung around my dad long enough to know what I was searching for. Our visits might have been few, but he'd always made them count. Mom thought we were taking drives to the park or the beach, but he'd been teaching me about his way of life, and introducing me to some people she wouldn't have approved of.

I pulled up to a garage on a darkened street corner. A light inside told me someone was around, even if the place wasn't officially open. My palms were sweating again but I blew out a breath and braced myself. It was time to put the socialite behind me and be every inch my father's daughter. I pulled the keys from the ignition and boldly walked inside.

"You can't be here, bitch," a voice said harshly from deep inside.

"I need to make a trade," I said.

A man with a leather cut strolled out of the garage, the lighting just good enough that I could read *Devil's Boneyard MC -- V.P. -- Scratch.*

I had no fucking clue if it was a rival club of Dixie Reapers or not and knew I needed to tread carefully. We studied one another, his gaze taking me in from head to toe. Not in an *I want to fuck her* kind of way, more like he was assessing if I was a threat.

"I have a problem," I said. "I have a hot car and need someone to take it off my hands. All I need in return is something that will run well enough for me to get a few states away."

Scratch rubbed his jaw and looked beyond me to the silver Mercedes.

"If you change out the VIN or strip it for parts, you can make a decent amount off it," I said. "I don't care what piece of shit you give me in return as long as it gets me where I'm going. I need reliable, not flashy."

He took in my appearance again. "You know how to ride?"

His question momentarily startled me. "Ride?"

He tipped his head and sauntered back inside the garage. Against my better judgment, I followed. There was an older motorcycle sitting off to the side. The pewter gray tank and fenders had seen better days, but as I circled the bike I saw that it was in pretty decent condition. The Harley emblem, though tarnished, was a welcome surprise. I wasn't a bike expert by any means, even though Dad had tried, but I thought it was a Harley Soft Tail, which meant it would be light enough for a woman like me to handle. Unlike the big monster my dad rode.

"How well does it run?" I asked.

Scratch walked over to a wall and pulled down a key, tossing it to me. I snatched it midair, straddled the bike and turned the key. Pulling out the choke, I pressed the start button and twisted the throttle. The engine rumbled, and I let it warm up for a few minutes before slowly feathering the choke back.

God, I'd fucking missed that sound. The thrum of the bike between my legs made me feel like I was coming home. Dad had taught me to ride when I was fourteen, and he'd rented a bike for me every time he'd visited after that, even if I hadn't been exactly been legal to drive the first few years.

"Even trade?" I asked.

The gaze Scratch gave me said he saw more than I liked, but he nodded.

"I just need to get my stuff from the Mercedes. It's unlocked," I said, handing him the car keys.

When I returned with my backpack strapped to me, my purse stuffed inside, he held out some papers to me. I glanced at them and saw it was everything I'd need to make the bike legal when I got to where I was going.

"I don't know who you belong to, baby girl, or what you're running from, but you don't fucking stop until you reach your man."

"You know who I am," I said softly.

"Picture's been all over the news tonight, statewide from what I hear. You don't appear all that unstable to me, but that family you're leaving... they're bad news. Richard Benton III is not a nice man."

"You know my stepdad?" I asked without thinking.

"Know of him. My crew won't have anything to do with the shit he's mixed up in."

I straddled the bike again and nodded.

"Who taught you to ride? Socialites like you don't know shit about bikes."

"I'm not a socialite. I'm a biker's daughter." And that was as much as I was going to tell him.

"You better run to Daddy, then, girl, because you have no idea the kind of trouble that's following you. I'll make that car of yours disappear. You been using credit cards?" Scratch asked.

"No. Cash only. I'm running low, but I think I can make it where I'm going."

"What about a phone?"

I hesitated. "Yeah, I have my cell phone."

Scratch held out his hand. "Trust me, baby girl. You don't want to keep that phone on you. Especially if Richard Benton III paid for it. They'll find you in no time."

Unease filled me, and I wondered if my stepdad had been tracking me all this time. Were the cops just moments away from coming to get me? I swung my backpack in front of me and unzipped it, removing my phone from my purse. I gave it to Scratch, and he pulled out the SIM card and battery before stomping the shit out of my phone and busting it to pieces.

"Get going, girl, and like I said, don't fucking stop."

"Thank you," I said softly. Revving the engine of the old Harley, I eased out of the garage and took off down the street. It wasn't long before I was flying on the highway and crossing the Alabama state line.

By the time I'd reached the Dixie Reapers compound, I ached from head to toe and felt near to collapsing. I'd been on the road for about ten hours, and the sky was already starting to lighten. My bike came to a stop outside the gates, and a Prospect sauntered forward.

"You lost, sweet thing?" he asked, flashing crooked teeth through the beginnings of a beard.

"Get Bull."

The man rocked back on his heels. "Bull's busy."

"He's not too busy to see me."

"Sure." He chuckled. "The man's balls deep in pussy, but I'm sure he'll just run right out here to see you."

I turned off the engine on the bike, swung my leg over the seat, and stalked forward, poking the asshole in the chest and giving him the fiercest look I could muster. My shoulders were thrown back, and I hoped I looked more intimidating than I was. "Look here, you piece of shit. You get Bull, and you fucking get him now."

The man grabbed my hand and twisted so that I went down on my knee, my arm behind me at an odd angle.

"I don't care who the fuck you think you are, bitch. You don't fucking touch me unless you're going to wrap your lips around my cock."

Booted steps drew near. "Is there a problem, Pete?"

"Just some fucking whore who insists on seeing Bull," the man said, twisting my arm a little more and making me cry out. "Fucking poked my chest and bowed up at me like she's fucking someone."

The man in the shadows chuckled. "Is that so?"

The boots came closer, and a dark head of hair appeared. The eyes that fastened on mine nearly took my breath away. I'd recognize those green eyes anywhere.

"Venom," I said softly.

His gaze narrowed. "Just who the fuck are you, sweetheart? Because I sure as hell don't remember you."

"I'm Ridley Johnson," I said, my voice almost a whisper as dots swam in front of my vision. If the Prospect turned my arm any more, it would break.

Surprise flashed in Venom's eyes, and he shot up to his full height. The crack of a fist filled the silence, and I was suddenly released. As I tumbled the rest of the way to the ground, strong arms wrapped around me.

"I've got you, baby girl," Venom murmured. "No one's going to fucking touch you again."

Venom lifted me into his arms, and I held on tight.

"Roll that bike up to the clubhouse," he barked at the Prospect.

"Who the hell is she?" the Prospect asked, his eyes burning with hate in the near darkness.

"Bull's daughter."

The Prospect's eyes widened, and he had that *I'm so fucked* look on his face.

The clubhouse was noisy, the air thick with smoke. Venom strode through the crowd, everyone looking at me in curiosity. He carried me down the hall and stopped at a door with his name on it. Somehow juggling me, he managed to pull out some keys from his pocket and unlocked it before stepping inside and kicking the door shut.

Venom eased me down onto a chair beside the bed and hunkered down in front of me. His gaze scanned my face and the rest of me, fury brewing in his gorgeous eyes when he saw the red marks on my arm from the Prospect.

"You wait here. I'm going to go get your daddy."

Without another word, he turned and stormed out of the room. As I slumped in the chair, I wondered if I'd made the right choice. I hadn't seen my daddy in so damn long. What if he wasn't happy to see me?

Chapter Two

Venom

I didn't know what the fuck had brought Ridley to the compound after all this time, but I figured it couldn't be good. And I sure as fuck wasn't going to think about how goddamn perfect she'd felt in my arms. Gone was the adorable cherub who had skipped around the clubhouse on family days. In her place was a stunning woman with curves in all the right places and legs for miles. Shit, even if my brother weren't her daddy, I was too damn old for someone like her. My dick wasn't getting the message.

I pressed my hand against my zipper hoping like I hell I didn't have a noticeable erection when I knocked on Bull's door. If he thought for one second I was lusting after his baby girl, he'd cut off my balls. My dick had hardened nearly to the point of pain just from holding her. The scent of the wind clinging to her, and something softer under that, had nearly made me do something stupid. Like throw her over my shoulder and carry her off to my house for a proper fucking. I could only imagine how damn hard I'd be if I ever had her naked. I'd lusted after women plenty of times, but I'd sure as fuck never felt like this. My inner caveman wanted me to roar that she was mine, fill her so full of my cum that everyone would damn well know it.

What the fuck? Get it together.

I didn't know what the hell was going on. I'd never felt like this before and sure as hell shouldn't be having these thoughts about Ridley-fucking-Johnson. The girl was young enough to be my daughter, but fuck if there was a single fatherly thought in my head when it came to her. One look in her eyes when that dumb shit Prospect had her on the ground, and I'd been a goner. I'd wanted to rip the fucker's arms off for hurting her. Those beautiful blue eyes that seemed to look right through me could bring me to my knees.

My dick pulsed in my pants as I thought about spreading her across my bed. I had no doubt I could spend hours between her thighs, until we were both exhausted and well-sated. I didn't understand why I wanted her so fucking much when I'd only held her in my arms briefly. Jesus, I was a fucking pussy, but I'd have gladly fallen to my knees and worshiped at her feet. I'd love nothing more than to spread those thighs wide and lick her until she screamed my name.

When my dick was under control, mostly, I knocked on Bull's door. The sounds coming from his room told me enough to know he was going to be pissed for the interruption. The man might be pushing fifty, but it didn't stop him from taking two to three club whores to his room each night. Often at the same time.

There was a growl on the other side of the door, and he jerked it open. I kept my gaze eye level because if there was anything I didn't want to see, it was Bull's cock. Mine never got any complaints, but the man hadn't gotten his name for nothing.

"What the fuck do you want, Venom?"

"Get dressed. We have a problem."

"It can fucking wait." He started to slam the door shut, but my hand whipped up and caught it.

"No, it can't fucking wait. Are you seriously going to brush off your VP?" I stared him down, and he finally relented. "Come to my room after you're dressed. And get those fucking sluts out of your room."

Bull nodded and shut the door. I blew out a breath and went back down to my room. My hand gripped the knob, but I hesitated. A woman's soft sobs could be heard from inside, and my gut twisted. I was a hard man, had done a lot of bad shit and gone through a lot of pain, but if there was one thing I couldn't handle, it was tears from the angel in my room. The moment I'd seen those blue eyes of hers, I'd been fucked.

Come on, asshole. Quit being a chickenshit.

I opened the door and stepped inside. Ridley blinked up at me, hastily wiping the tears from her cheeks. My gaze caressed every inch of her, and I had to admit I was surprised. She was hot as fucking hell, but I would have expected Bull's daughter to show up in some sort of designer clothes. The boots on her feet looked new, but she looked every inch a biker's woman. It made her hot as fuck, and my dick surged again.

"Your dad will be here in a minute," I told her.

She sniffled and nodded, her gaze staying on mine.

"How'd you know it was me out at the gate?" I asked. It had been too damn dark for her to see my patch.

Ridley smiled faintly. "You haven't changed much in the last fourteen years. Besides, Dad always showed me pictures on his phone of everyone when he visited."

I ran my hands through my hair, remembering that I'd found some silver threaded through it recently. I'd been clean-shaven back when I'd known Ridley and now kept a short beard. And I sure as fuck hadn't had lines around my eyes when I'd last seen her. She might think I hadn't changed much, but the man who looked back in the mirror every damn morning said otherwise.

Her eyes twinkled as she looked me over. "You know, when I was little, I used to tell my daddy I was going to grow up and marry you."

I gave a bark of laughter. "Why the hell would you have wanted to marry me?"

She shrugged. "Even when I was five I felt this pull toward you. You were always nice to me, and I had a crush on you. Well, as much as a five-year-old can have. You were larger than life, and the few times you ever hugged me I always felt safe."

A knot formed in my throat at her words.

"You were something special, baby girl. Still are."

A knock sounded at the door and I let Bull in. The moment his gaze landed on his daughter, his eyes went wide and he froze in place.

"Hi, Daddy," she said quietly. "I'm in trouble."

Bull moved farther into the room, and I shut the door. Until we knew what was going on, there wasn't any point in every nosy person in the clubhouse hearing about it. Something told me that Ridley would want privacy for whatever she had to say. I couldn't imagine anything making her run from the life she knew. Who the hell gave up living in a mansion to come to a biker compound?

Bull stood in front of her, a hand slowly reached out, but he pulled back at the last minute. Ridley stared up at him. When he didn't move again, I saw the tears gather in her eyes.

"You stupid shit, she thinks you don't want her here," I said with a growl.

That seemed to give Bull a jolt, and he gathered his girl in his arms.

"I'm so sorry, Daddy," Ridley said as she cried against her dad's shoulder. "I should have called even if Mom wouldn't let me see you, but I was too scared you wouldn't want anything to do with me. She told me what she said. I never told her I didn't want to see you."

"What did she do to you?" Bull asked.

"It doesn't matter now." Ridley sniffled again. "But they're really angry with me. They plastered my face all over the news and said I'm unstable. If they find out I'm here, they'll come for me."

"I'd like to see them fucking try," I muttered.

Ridley eased back down into the chair and stared up at us. "You may not want me to stay here. I'm going to bring all sorts of trouble to your door."

"Baby girl, trouble is what we specialize in," I said with a smile.

"Have either of you ever heard of Fernando Montoya?"

The blood froze in my veins as I stared at her. What the fuck did she know about that piece of shit? The thought that Montoya had even ever laid eyes on her made me want to go fucking insane. Bull looked my way, and I knew he was just as worried as I was. If Ridley coming here had anything to do with that asshole, then things were way fucking worse than I'd imagined.

"What do you know about Montoya?" I asked, trying to keep my voice calm.

Ridley looked like she was going to cry again, but she took a shuddering breath and pulled herself together. She might be fucking scared, but her standoff with the Prospect at the gate told me she had guts. If Montoya had anything to do with her showing up here, then she was going to have to be a fighter whether she wanted to be or not.

"Yesterday was my birthday and I had planned to sneak away. My friends helped me arrange it. I was supposedly going out to party with them, but really I was going to drive straight here. I was so damn tired of the shit my mom and Richard pull, and I knew I needed to get out."

"Happy birthday, angel," I said.

She gave me a wan smile. "About an hour before I was supposed to leave, Mom came to my room and told me plans had changed. I was to shower and dress in an outfit she'd chosen because my stepdad had someone important coming to dinner."

"Montoya?" Bull asked.

Ridley nodded. "They introduced me as I came down the stairs, and the cold look in his eyes made my skin crawl. It was like he was imagining me without my clothes, but his eyes were just so empty. Then at dinner, Mom made me sit by him. He kept touching me and then... "

My blood was absolutely boiling, and I wanted to hunt the fucker down and rip off his hands for daring to touch her.

"And then what?" Bull asked, sounding far calmer than I was.

"He... touched me."

"You already said he touched you," I said.

Her cheeks flushed. "No, I mean... he put his hand all the way up my dress and touched me... somewhere else."

Motherfucker! I growled and put my fist through the damn wall.

"I bolted out of the dining room saying I needed to use the bathroom. The vent in the downstairs bathroom somehow connects to the dining room. If people are in there, you can hear everything they say," she said.

"What did they say, baby?" Bull asked.

"Mom and Richard were selling me to Montoya." Tears filled her eyes again. "He talked about needing to fully check out the merchandise and have a sample before buying. Said he was going to break me in and train me properly before… "

Bull began pacing furiously. I flexed my hand, my knuckles split from going through the sheetrock. The ache in my hand was mild compared to what Ridley had been through. If her whore of a mother and that sick fuck she'd married had promised Ridley to Montoya, there was no doubt he would demand they follow through. Which meant it was only a matter of time before Ridley's mom and stepass showed up on our doorstep. It wouldn't take them long to figure out that Ridley had come home.

I smiled at the thought of getting my hands on those two. If they did come here, it would be the last place they ever visited. The compound had a special spot for unwanted visitors. There was an old barn at the back of the property, far enough away from all the homes that if people screamed as they begged for their lives, no one would hear them.

Fuck if I would ever let Montoya get his hands on Ridley. And I knew the MC would have my back. She was family, even if she hadn't been here in fourteen years. Those who had been around back then would remember her, and the others would fall in line just because she was Bull's daughter. We took care of our own.

While Bull paced and pulled at his hair, I knelt in front of Ridley. Taking her soft hand in mine, I stared into her eyes, letting her see the conviction in mine.

"No one is going to hurt you. We'll deal with the threat, but for now, you're safe here."

Bull stopped. "She can't stay here."

Ridley's eyes widened as she stared at her dad.

"There's no room for her at the clubhouse, and even if someone gave up their room for her, I don't want her here around all the shit that goes down," Bull said.

Ridley looked from her dad to me. "Then where am I supposed to go?"

Bull's gaze focused on me. "You take her home. You'll protect her."

I shot to my feet. Yeah, I fucking wanted to protect her, but putting Ridley under my roof was like asking the fox to guard the henhouse. I'd gotten hard just carrying her in from the gate, and Bull wanted me to share a house with her? Was the man fucking insane? Touching her would be all kinds of wrong and start trouble. I'd never wanted to fuck someone so badly in my life, and I had a feeling that once I'd had a taste of Ridley, I'd never let her go.

But what if it's all kinds of right?

No. I couldn't take her home with me. I wouldn't.

Her bright blue eyes stared at me, complete trust shining in their depths, and I knew I was well and truly fucked. How the hell do you say no to an angel? Especially one as gorgeous as Ridley.

"Fine. She can stay with me."

I had a feeling I'd just damned myself to hell. Blue balls were going to be the least of my problems.

Chapter Three

Ridley

When Venom said he was taking me home, I hadn't realized he lived at the compound, but in an actual house. I'd remember some houses scattered around the place when I'd visited as a child, but I'd never been in one. Venom's house was spacious with a large wraparound porch, and not at all where I imagined him living. This house was cute and screamed family, with its crisp white paint and blue shutters, but as far as I knew, Venom was single and had never had kids. Of course, not having talked to Dad in the last year, and not having seen him for a year longer, I was no longer up to date on what happened around the Dixie Reapers MC. He never shared sacred things, like the jobs they went on or how they made their money, but he would always tell me the antics the guys got up to, or who was seriously seeing someone.

For some reason, I didn't like the thought of Venom having an old lady. I tried not to analyze it too much. He was just a friend of my dad's, a brother, and he was helping me because I was family. Reading anything more into it than that would just get me into trouble. Besides, Venom was a lot older than me and probably just saw me as a pesky kid. Still, whenever Dad had mentioned Venom over the years, a surge of jealousy had hit me whenever he was with a woman. Dad had shown me pictures of the guys on his phone at every visit, and once I'd hit the age of fourteen, I'd started seeing Venom differently from everyone else.

It wasn't so much that he was gorgeous, because there was a roughness to him, but he had the kind of masculine beauty that made me weak in the knees. He was rugged and manly, and a far cry from the guys I'd dated. Even when I'd wondered if I'd never see him again, I'd still wanted him. Oh, I'd hoped to one day return to the Dixie Reapers, had even made plans, but until I'd actually arrived at the gates I hadn't known if it would ever really happen. But now my schoolgirl crush had turned into something else. As I watched the way his jeans hugged his ass, I couldn't help but wonder if he looked just as good out of them.

The porch steps creaked as Venom's boots clomped up them. He'd given me a ride on the back of his bike, and mine was still parked in front of the clubhouse. As vast as the compound was, I'd have liked to have had it closer in case I wanted to go for a ride. The Dixie Reapers owned over five hundred acres, every last square foot enclosed with a ten-foot fence topped with barbed wire. I'd never thought about it before, but it must have taken some serious money to pull off something like that. Whatever they did to get paid, it must pay well. My dad had never flashed huge amounts of cash, unlike Richard, but he'd also made sure I always had whatever I needed. Until Mom had put a stop to it.

Venom unlocked the door and ushered me inside. The place smelled like him, and I almost closed my eyes and took a deep breath. A lamp was burning in the living room off to our right. A large, leather sectional dominated the room, along with a matching recliner, and a TV so big it must be like sitting in a theater when he played movies. Despite my stepdad's wealth, there hadn't been a lot of TVs in the house, and none that extravagant. They'd decided TV was bad for you. I nearly snorted at the thought, considering what they'd planned for me. Apparently human trafficking was all right, just not electronics.

"Living room, dining room, kitchen, a half bath, and a game room are downstairs," Venom said. "All the bedrooms and full baths are upstairs."

"I know I'm cramping your style, but thanks for letting me stay."

His lips twitched. "I don't bring women here, so it's fine."

Right. His room at the clubhouse was probably used for that. I wasn't stupid enough to think a man who looked like Venom didn't have his choice of women. I didn't like the idea of him and the club sluts. They were just so trashy, and he seemed like the type of guy who should be above that kind of thing. Even though I hadn't seen him since I was just a kid, I'd heard enough about him through my dad over the years that I felt like I knew Venom.

And it hadn't escaped my notice that he was easy on the eyes. That thick dark hair of his had just a sprinkling of silver mixed in, and while I'd never really gone for guys with beards, he was sexy with one. And the man had muscles for days. When he'd carried me from the gate, I'd felt safe. Protected. I wasn't sure how much of that was left over from the hero worship I'd felt toward him as a kid, and how much was just a woman appreciating a strong man.

"I'll show you to your room," he said. "You look like you're about to drop."

I followed him up the stairs, and we passed several doors before he stopped at the end of the hall. He shoved the door open, and I stepped inside. The furniture was a warm maple, the walls an icy blue. A quilt in muted blues, greens, and yellows covered the queen-size bed. There weren't any curtains or pictures. The wide slat blinds let in the morning light as the sun began to rise.

"I'm sure you're used to something far grander than this," Venom said.

"It's a beautiful room." And it really was. I didn't just love the colors, but I loved what it represented to me. Freedom. As long as I stayed in this room, it meant my mom and stepdad -- or Mr. Montoya -- couldn't get their hands on me. My dad wouldn't have sent me with Venom if he didn't think I'd be safe.

"Bathroom is across the hall. I'm sure you'd love to shower and rest after your long trip," Venom said.

Part of me longed to lie down, but my nerves were still all knotted up, and I wasn't certain I could sleep if I tried. I knew my dad wouldn't let anything happen to me, and he must feel Venom would protect me too, but it didn't stop me from dreading my family finding me here. Even if they couldn't physically remove me from the property, it didn't mean they wouldn't cause trouble. And if I was too much trouble, what if the club decided to hand me over to my family? Not that I really considered Mom and my stepdad family at this point. Family didn't sell you to a cold man who wanted to do horrible things to you.

Venom stayed in the doorway a moment, watching me, then he moved farther down the hall. I heard a door open and shut, and once more I felt completely alone. I shrugged out of my backpack and emptied the contents on the bed. I only had two changes of clothes inside, and nothing to sleep in. I hadn't counted on all my money being about gone when I'd reached my destination and had thought I'd buy more clothes when I got here. Now I didn't know what the hell I was going to do. Was it even safe for me to go out somewhere and shop?

I took a clean pair of panties out of the pile of clothes and dumped everything else in the empty dresser. Stepping into the hall, I stared at what I thought was Venom's bedroom door, hesitating only a moment before going to knock. He jerked it open, and my heart stuttered. My wide gaze took in the shirtless wonder of Venom's broad shoulders and muscular chest. My fingers twitched with the urge to reach out and touch him, but I refrained -- barely.

"Did you need something, Ridley?"

"Um, yeah. I don't have anything to sleep in. Could I borrow a shirt?"

He arched an eyebrow, but shoved away from the door and walked over to a dresser. Pulling open a drawer, he withdrew a black tee with *Dixie Reapers MC* across the front and tossed it to me. I snatched it out of the air, mumbled a thank-you, and darted into the bathroom. I slammed the door shut and leaned against it, my heart racing. I'd seen bare-chested men plenty of times, so why did Venom's large pectorals make my knees weak and make me want to do something stupid, like plaster myself to him and beg him to take me to bed? He was just a guy. A much older guy.

A hot-as-fuck guy.

He probably thought I was some stupid girl. I groaned and closed my eyes in embarrassment. I'd run away like a chicken, bolted instead of facing him and the desire I couldn't deny. I was nineteen, not five. I'd had boyfriends, but I hadn't gone much past kissing with any of them, had never felt the urge. But one look from a halfway undressed Venom, and I'd been ready to drop my panties. What the hell was wrong with me? If he knew how I felt, he would probably laugh.

I set the tee and my panties on the bathroom counter before pulling the shower door open and turning on the water. I dragged the ponytail holder out of my hair and finger-combed it, but the snarls from riding the bike were just too much. I winced as the tangled strands pulled at my scalp, and dug through the bathroom drawers in search of a brush. I found one that had never been opened. Ripping the cardboard off it, I ran it through my long hair until it was tangle-free.

When I stepped under the hot spray, I hoped that it would wash away the last twelve hours. I used the shampoo and soap Venom had provided for his guests to scrub myself clean, but I still felt dirty. That man had touched me. His fingers had stroked between my legs like he had a right to me. I felt sick just thinking about it. I hadn't even allowed my past boyfriends to touch me there, and now some sick creep had violated me.

I knew it could have been much worse, would have been if I had stuck around. But I didn't like that he had made me feel so helpless. My body began to shake as I thought about what had almost happened to me, and my legs gave out. I crashed to the bottom of the tub, my shoulder slamming into the glass door, making it pop open. I wrapped my arms around myself, as if maybe I could hold the pieces together because I felt like I was breaking. A sob tore from my throat and then another.

I'd always wondered if my mother loved me, had thought many times she'd only taken me as a way to get back at my dad. But to know that she'd planned to give me away, to force me into being a whore, it chilled me. She'd never been warm, never been much for hugs, but I would have never thought her capable of such a thing. The Mercedes, the jewelry, the trips to Paris... I wondered now if she'd done all those things to make herself feel better. How long had she planned to do this to me?

The water shut off, and I blinked up at Venom through blurry eyes. He'd stepped into the shower, barefoot and only wearing jeans. The denim was wet now and molded to his thighs as he crouched in front of me. I should have been embarrassed over my naked state, but it bothered me more that he'd seen me so weak, crying in the shower like a lost little girl. And maybe I was.

"You're safe," he said, his voice deep and smooth as whiskey.

"He touched me. He..." I swallowed hard. "No one's ever touched me like that before. It shouldn't have been him."

Venom muttered something under his breath, then he wrapped a towel around me and swung me up into his arms. He set me down on the bathroom counter and grabbed another towel. Briskly, he dried my hair and my body. I hadn't even realized until that moment that I was cold.

"You've never been touched before?" he asked.

"No," I admitted softly. My cheeks warmed. "I guess a nineteen-year-old virgin sounds stupid, but I was saving myself. Now I wish I hadn't."

"Better to wait than end up with the wrong guy."

"Maybe, but now I can't get it out of my head. The way his hand felt as he stroked me. It was wrong, and it makes me feel so sick."

Venom tipped my chin up, his gaze burning into me. "What can I do, angel? What do you need to make it all better?"

"Take away the memories?" I asked softly. I knew he'd never do it, would never touch me. As Bull's daughter, and at least twenty years his junior, I knew I was untouchable in his mind, but I couldn't hold the words back.

Venom stared at me, hard, but I didn't have a clue what he was thinking. His eyes gave nothing away. He reached for the towel draped around me and dropped it to the floor before lifting me into his arms again. With long strides, he walked down the hall to his bedroom, kicking the door shut behind him. His bed was unmade, and he dropped me in the center of the tangled blankets.

His gaze caressed every inch of me, and I didn't try to hide from him. The way he looked at me made me feel alive and on fire. An ache began to build inside me, and I felt my pussy grow slick. No one had ever watched me with such intensity before, such desire. I could see the heat in his eyes, the need burning in their depths. I wanted this, wanted him, whatever he was willing to give me. I didn't know what to expect, but I wasn't afraid.

"I'll make you feel good, baby girl. But that's as far as things can go between us. I'm not the kind of man you should give yourself to completely. Your dad's going to have my balls for laying a hand on you, but I can't stand that look in your eyes. I'll chase away the demons, baby."

He crawled onto the bed, despite the soaked denim clinging to him, his hands sliding up my legs, spreading them. His body covered mine, his weight pressing me into the mattress. I could feel the hard ridge of his cock through his jeans, and I wanted to beg him to take them off. His lips caressed mine, slowly, almost tenderly. The whiskers on his face were softer than I'd have expected as they brushed against me.

Venom's tongue stroked my lower lip, and I opened to him. His kiss was slow and deep, as if he wanted to savor the moment. He tasted of whiskey and smoke, and I craved more. His lips left mine, trailing down my throat. He gave me a gentle nip that had me sucking in a breath and my toes curling, then he licked the sting away. Some part of me wished he would mark me. I wanted people to know that I'd been his, if even for a little while. I'd never wanted that before, never wanted to be consumed by someone, but I would gladly give myself over to Venom. He was so strong, so sure of himself. He was nothing like the boys I'd dated, but was all man.

His lips closed over the tip of my breast, his teeth grazing my nipple as he drew it into his mouth. I cried out as pleasure shot straight to my clit. He sucked hard, until I thought I might come just from that. My nipple throbbed and ached when he released it, only to latch onto the other side. He took his time, driving my need for him higher and higher, and he still hadn't touched me where I wanted him most. I felt hot and trembled with need, and hoped he'd soon ease the ache.

Venom worked his way down my body until his shoulders were spreading my thighs wide. He stared, licking his lips. My breath caught, and I wondered what would happen next. He'd told me that he'd give me pleasure, and he had, but he'd also made my need for him grow until I was nearly ready to beg him for release. I'd made myself come a few times, but something told me that being with Venom would be different. Vastly different.

His finger stroked over the lips of my pussy.

"You're so damn wet, baby."

His finger dipped inside me, sliding into my tight channel. He thrust in and out several times, before adding a second finger. I felt myself stretch around the digits and couldn't help but moan. I'd never felt anything like it before. My body was hyperaware of Venom, and my clit was throbbing. He continued sliding his fingers in and out. His gaze was fastened between my legs, a look of hunger on his face, as he watched his fingers moving in and out of me.

He added a third finger, and it burned a little as he stretched me farther. He seemed content to watch his fingers fucking me, but I wanted more. The ache inside me was growing with every stroke, and I whimpered with need. Venom's gaze flicked up and clashed with mine. His eyes had darkened, and he looked like he wanted to possess me. He leaned forward and blew across my clit before his tongue flicked out to tease the bud. I cried out at the contact and wanted to beg for more.

Venom's tongue lapped at me as his fingers worked me harder and deeper. I could feel something building inside me and knew in that moment the brief bits of pleasure I'd found alone in my bedroom at night were nothing compared to this. He growled as he sucked my clit, and the vibration pushed me over the edge. I cried out his name, pleasure pulsing through me from head to toe. His lips released me, but his fingers kept sliding in and out of me, as if he were trying to wring every drop of pleasure from me.

"Fuck. You have no idea how much I want to see this sweet pussy wrapped around my cock. I want to stretch you wide while I fuck you deep."

I trembled at his words, wanting that more than anything.

"You're so damn wet, baby girl. So fucking tight. You came so hard you drenched the bed. I fucking love it."

"Venom, please," I begged.

He sucked my clit again, his tongue thrashing against it. His fingers never slowed as he pulled another orgasm from me. It felt different than when I'd made myself come, stronger and more intense, and yet

I still wanted more. I wanted to know what it felt like to have a man inside me, to have Venom stretching me and taking me. I wanted him to possess every inch of me.

His fingers slid free of my body, and he licked them clean. "You taste so damn good."

"Venom, I want…"

"You want what, baby girl?"

"More. I want to feel you inside me."

He shook his head and stood up. "Not a good idea."

"Why not?"

"Because if I take you, your innocence won't be the only thing I claim. I'm going to want to take you hard, and deep. And I'll take you fucking bare because I can't think of anything I want more than to see my cum on you, marking you as mine."

His words turned me on so damn much. I wanted him to claim to me, to mark me, but I could tell from the stubborn set of his chin that he was determined it wouldn't happen. I slid off the bed and fell to my knees in front of him. The button on his jeans was already undone, and I pulled the zipper down. Venom didn't stop me, but his gaze stayed steady on me. I worked his wet jeans and boxer briefs down his thighs until his cock sprang free.

I'd never seen one in person before, but his seemed perfect to me. Hard, long, and wider than I'd imagined. I groaned, remembering his words. Yeah, he'd stretch me wide all right, and my pussy pulsed with need as I thought about feeling him inside me. I licked my lips and wrapped my fingers around his shaft. His skin was warm and smooth. My tongue flicked out and lapped up some pre-cum on the tip of his cock. The salty taste made my mouth water, and I went back for more, opening my mouth wide and taking as much of him as I could.

I licked and sucked his shaft, hoping I was doing it right. His fingers pried my hand away from his cock, and his hand fisted in my hair, drawing my head back.

"Tip your head and relax your throat," he said, his voice a near growl.

I did as he instructed, and Venom thrust his cock forward. His hips flexed, his cock working farther and farther into my mouth, until I felt him easing down my throat.

"Breathe through your nose, baby girl, and let me in. You know you want all this cock."

My hands gripped his thighs as he thrust deeper. I nearly gagged the first few times, then got the hang of it. Venom fucked my mouth with hard strokes, his cock plunging between my lips again and again. He seemed to grow harder, to swell even more. My mouth was taking all of him now, and he grunted his pleasure.

"Gonna come, baby girl. Swallow it. All of it."

I braced myself, and a few strokes later I felt the warm splash of his cum on my tongue. I swallowed, and more filled my mouth. He came hard, stream after stream, and I swallowed every last drop. Venom's cock thrust a few more times between my lips before he pulled free, breathing heavily. My lips felt swollen and my jaw ached, but I loved that I'd pleased him.

I stared at his cock and noticed he was still pretty damn hard for someone who had come so much. My eyes widened when it seemed to stiffen even more, getting longer. I'd thought men only recovered that fast in porn movies. I didn't know what to do and looked up at Venom for guidance.

"You have a choice to make, baby girl. You can get up and go back to your room right now, and I won't come after you. This can be a one-time thing. Or you can open that pretty mouth and take my cock again. And when you're done, I'll make you scream my name until you're hoarse. But that's all we can have. I won't claim you."

Go back to my lonely room? Even if I wanted more than he was willing to give, I wasn't stupid. Having part of him, sharing something like this with him, was better than not having anything. If it meant he'd only fuck my mouth, then so be it. I'd rather have the taste of his cum on my tongue than have nothing.

My jaw dropped, and I worked my way down his length. He groaned and murmured my name as he fisted my hair again, driving his cock deeper. I didn't know if what we had could last more than just this one day, but I was going to take everything he was willing to give me. I wanted Venom, any way I could have him.

Chapter Four

Venom

Ridley was pretty damn amazing. She'd sucked me off four times throughout the day, getting a little bit better each time. Most women couldn't take all of me, but fuck if my cock didn't slide down her throat with ease. I'd wanted more, so much more, but I wasn't a big enough bastard to take what I wanted. She'd screamed my name until she'd grown hoarse. I sucked her pretty little clit and fucked her with my fingers until she'd gotten too sore to play anymore. Any other woman and I'd have told them to get the fuck out of my bed when I was done with them, but Ridley was different. She was nothing like the club whores I'd fucked in my younger days as a Prospect, before I'd figured out I didn't want sloppy seconds or thirds, or the more experienced women I picked up in bars now. Hell, the way she'd stared at me when she'd pulled down my pants, I was pretty certain she'd never seen a cock before.

I'd held her for hours, just enjoying the feel of her in my arms. We'd taken breaks to eat and get some rest, but even now my mouth watered at the thought of tasting her sweet pussy again. My phone had been buzzing off and on for a while now, and if I had to guess, I'd say it was Bull. I hadn't looked at the damn thing, not wanting to interrupt my time with the angel in my arms. I knew her daddy was going to castrate me if he found out what I'd been doing with his daughter, but death was a small price to pay all things considered.

My phone buzzed again and I picked it up, checking the screen. *Bull.* He was going to want to know why I hadn't been answering my phone, and I didn't think he wanted to hear that I'd been making his daughter come all over my face for hours on end. And damn could the girl come! She'd soaked the bed with how much her pretty pussy flooded with each release. I'd love to feel all that cream coating my cock as I drove into her.

I glanced at Ridley lying beside me. She was pressed against my side, her head in the crook of my shoulder. My hand rested at her waist, her skin warm and soft under my rough fingers. I answered the phone as it started to buzz again, and hoped like hell I didn't wake her up. She was exhausted and deserved some sleep.

"What?" I barked into the phone.

"You may be my VP, but that's my daughter you took home, asshole."

"I'm aware of that." It was about the only thing that had kept me from being balls deep in her pussy. Well, that was one reason. The other was that she deserved so much better than me. Her first time should be sweet and tender, and I didn't have a damn clue how to do sweet and tender. I'd take her hard and deep, and fucking pound her pussy until I filled her with my cum.

"Should I call Zipper?" Bull asked. I didn't like that he'd brought up the club's tattooist.

"What the fuck would you call him for?"

"Because I came by earlier to check on my little girl and heard her screaming your fucking name. Since you've claimed her, I figured you'd want her inked."

Oh, shit.

"I didn't claim her," I said.

Bull snorted. "Didn't sound that way to me."

"She wanted me to take away the bad memories of Montoya, but my cock didn't get inside her." *Except for that luscious mouth.*

"I don't fucking care," Bull screamed into the phone. "If I'd thought you'd put your hands on her the first chance you had her alone, I never would have sent her home with you. I trusted you to take care of her, to protect her."

I'd taken care of her all right, just not in the way her daddy approved.

"Ridley is a grown fucking woman," I told him. "I gave her what she needed. She knew things weren't going further, and she accepted that. And you don't dare question whether or not I'd protect her." Bull didn't know it, but I'd lay down my life for the woman in my arms.

"She's nineteen for Christ sake!"

"She's still a woman, Bull. A young one, but full-grown just the same, and she can make her own decisions about her life. She doesn't need Daddy's permission to have sex."

Bull started cursing again, then grew quiet.

"I talked to Torch. There's been a new development. He said he's calling church, so you need to get your ass over here. Bring Ridley with you. She can sit at the bar, and the Prospects can keep an eye on her."

I hung up and looked at my phone, noticing the four missed calls and one text from the Pres. Fuck. Torch was going to be pissed I hadn't picked up, and I doubt he'd care that I'd been busy making Ridley scream my name. I stroked her cheek and pressed my lips to hers. She moaned and leaned in closer.

"Come on, angel. Time to get up."

Her eyes fluttered open, and she gave me a sleepy smile.

"The Pres has called church, so I've gotta go. And you're going with me."

"I'm allowed in church?" she asked.

"No, but you can sit at the bar. Go get dressed. I'll wait for you by the front door."

Ridley rolled out of bed and disappeared down the hall, and yeah, I fucking admit it. I admired her ass as she walked away. Damn if I didn't stay hard around that woman. A shower would have been nice, since I smelled like sex, but there wasn't time. I grabbed a fresh pair of boxer briefs and jeans from the dresser, slid on my cut, and jammed my feet into my boots. Ridley met me at the front door, and we rode over to the clubhouse. Her hands clutched my waist, and her body molded to my back. I'd always had a strict policy about no women on the back of my bike, even though I'd broken that rule last night. That shit was reserved for my old lady, if I ever took one. But Ridley felt like she fucking belonged there. She was made to ride a bike. *My bike.*

Two Prospects were on the porch of the clubhouse when we pulled up. They looked alert, their gazes scanning the area, and I wondered what had happened. Bull had mentioned a new development, and I suddenly wasn't quite as content as I had been moments before. If someone even thought of taking Ridley, I'd fucking end them. No one was taking her, not while there was breath in my lungs. I didn't usually pack heat around the compound unless I knew something was going down, but I was starting to wish I'd armed myself to the teeth. It wasn't like someone would ever get inside unless we allowed it to happen, but I wasn't going to take any chances with Ridley. She was too damn important to me.

Fuck. She'd been back in my life for not even a full day, and already I wanted her in every way possible. If I didn't think she could do so much better than me, nothing would have stopped me from getting balls deep inside her and branding her as mine. She was like the sun, all light and sweet, and my soul was as fucking dark as they came. I was tainted from the sins of my past, and those I'd yet to commit.

Ridley slipped her hand into mine, and I looked down at her in surprise. I'd never held a woman's hand before, had always shaken them off, but I tightened my grip and kept her close. We approached the bar, and I lifted her onto a stool. She smiled up at me, even though I could see the worry in her eyes. Not giving a fuck who saw, I leaned forward and kissed her hard. Ridley was mine, and yet she wasn't. I wasn't good for her, but it didn't stop me from wanting to brand her as my woman.

"I'll be back. Order a drink."

Her nose wrinkled. "I'm under twenty-one."

My lips twitched as I fought not to smile. "Baby girl, we don't exactly play by the rules around here. You want a drink, order one. You think anyone gives a fuck how old you are?"

The Prospect behind the bar approached, jerking his head down the hall. "Everyone's already in there. I'll keep an eye on her."

"If she gets so much as a paper cut while I'm gone, I'll beat the fucking hell out of you."

He nodded, and his lips firmed. I knew he'd watch over her, lay down his life for her if the need arose. It was one thing, knowing she was Bull's daughter, but now the club knew she meant something to me too. I was so fucking screwed. She was in my bed, on my bike, and I was openly kissing her in the clubhouse. My dick might not have gotten anywhere near her pussy, but I might as well have pissed on her leg like a dog marking its territory.

I pulled myself away from Ridley before I tossed her over my shoulder and carried her to the nearest bed. When I saw the closed doors, I wondered if they'd started church without me. I barged in, letting the doors slam shut behind me. All talking ceased, and the Pres gave me a glare that would have made a lesser man cower. I sprawled in my seat, ignoring the pointed glare from Bull. Every patched member was present, and a few were smirking. It left little doubt that Bull had been complaining about me defiling his daughter.

"Your phone broke?" Torch asked.

"No, Pres. I was otherwise occupied."

"Fucking my daughter," Bull said, spit flying from his mouth. "He was supposed to be protecting her."

"Can't think of any safer place for her to be than in my bed," I drawled.

Bull rose from his seat, fists clenched at his sides. "You're just using her like all the other whores you take to your bed."

His words made my anger ignite. "Did you just compare Ridley to a whore?"

Torch steepled his fingers in front of him and watched me carefully. I could almost see the wheels turning in his head. His gaze strayed to Bull, and he motioned for my brother to have a seat.

"Before we continue down this enlightening path," Torch said, "we need to discuss a few things. I called church because Bull's daughter has returned to us, and she's in trouble. Her mother and stepdad have offered her to Fernando Montoya as payment, for what we've yet to determine. It seems they're doing their best to track her down, and they're getting closer than I'd like. I guess that stupid bitch mother of hers didn't think she'd come running to Daddy after the crap she pulled last year, otherwise they'd already be at our gates demanding we hand her over."

"What do you mean they're getting close?" I asked.

"Ridley apparently had her cell phone with her for most of her journey. She stopped at a small town outside the panhandle, and that's where the Bentons lost her trail. Now, normally I wouldn't have thought much about it, but that unassuming little town is home of the Devil's Boneyard MC," Torch said.

"Taught my girl everything I know," Bull said. "She was smart and found a chop shop to ditch her Mercedes."

Torch nodded. "I called Cinder and asked if anyone knew anything. She took the car to their chop shop and their VP put her on the bike. He also helped her destroy her phone. Now the good news is that they can't track her anymore, and I was assured that car has been taken care of. But the fact she was coming to Alabama is probably going to tip off her mom that she came here. Might not be long before they show up here."

"Has contact been made from her mom?" I asked.

"Not yet. I'm hoping they don't show up for a while. I've asked Wire to do a little digging for us. I want to know everything about Richard Benton III, and I want to know his connection to Montoya. Wire is going to start with Benton's bank records and business dealings, and we'll go from there. I'm hoping we can find some leverage," Torch said.

"So what do you want us to do for now?" Flicker asked.

"Ridley has to stay at the compound," Torch said. "Venom was chosen to protect her."

Bull's face turned red, and his fist slammed down on the table.

Torch raised a brow. "Obviously, Bull is reconsidering that decision."

"Ridley isn't going anywhere," I said.

"The fuck you say?" Bull shot to his feet. "I won't leave her under your care when you're going to treat her like trash. You didn't pick her up on the damn street corner. She's not here for your amusement."

My chair scraped the floor as I stood, my body trembling from my barely controlled rage. That's twice he'd compared Ridley to a whore, and I wasn't going to fucking stand for it. Yeah, I'd pleasured her in my bed, but I'd done it to take care of her, because she'd asked me to make the memories go away. I never would have fucking touched her if she hadn't asked. But now that I had, now that her taste was still on my tongue, I would be damned if anyone was taking her out of my house.

"Ridley isn't going anywhere," I said, my teeth clenching from the effort to not lay Bull out with one fucking punch. I didn't think Ridley would take it too well if I beat the shit out of her dad. And her opinion was about the only one that mattered right now.

"Venom," Torch said softly. "What is Ridley to you?"

My jaw clenched tighter until I thought my teeth might crack.

"Are you claiming her?" Torch asked.

"She deserves better," I muttered.

Torch studied me a moment, then snapped his fingers at our enforcer, Tank. "Bring the girl here."

I sank into my chair and tried to calm my racing heart. Why the hell was he asking for Ridley? No one came to church except patched members. Had I put her in danger with the attention I'd given her? Torch was fucking stone-cold, and if he thought for one second that Ridley was going to cause problems within the club, I didn't doubt that he'd boot her out. But if Ridley left, I was going with her. Brotherhood be damned, I wasn't going to leave her defenseless when there were monsters waiting to snatch her up.

Tank re-entered the room, his hand gripping Ridley's arm and practically dragging her inside. I gripped the arms of my chair tight to keep from going to her. She stared at everyone, wide-eyed, and looked scared as hell. I wanted to wrap my baby girl in my arms and tell her everything would be fine.

"Ridley, do you remember me?" Torch asked.

She hesitantly nodded. "You're the president of the Dixie Reapers."

"That's right. And the man beside me is my VP."

Her glaze clashed with mine.

"I understand that Bull sent you home with Venom when you arrived. Did you go with him willingly?" Torch asked.

"Yes," Ridley said.

"And anything that happened while you were there was consensual? He didn't force himself on you in any way?"

"Venom would never hurt me," she said.

"If you had your choice, would you want to remain with Venom? Or would you prefer to move to another house? I could even arrange for your dad to stay with you," Torch said.

Her gaze met mine again and held. It was like she was looking to me for answers, but I couldn't say anything. This had to be her choice. I might wish that I could claim every sexy inch of her, but she was still a free woman. She didn't wear my brand, or anyone else's. And once the threat to her life was over, I imagined she'd move on and put the Dixie Reapers in her rearview mirror. And me. She'd walk away from me, and that's why I couldn't take things as far as I wanted.

"Ridley, I'm asking you, not Venom," Torch said.

"I want to stay with Venom," she said softly. "If that's okay with him."

Fuck yes, it's okay with me!

"Ridley, I know you came to us because your father is here," Torch said. "But I need to know if you plan to stay even after the danger has passed. There's not a lot of room in our club for women. You're either a club slut or an old lady, and right now, you aren't either."

"If staying is an option, I think I'd like to," she said. "But I could never be a club slut."

"You don't have a problem wearing someone's brand?" Flicker asked.

"What's a brand? Like you literally burn a brand into my skin?" she asked, her face paling.

"This is ridiculous," Bull said. "My daughter isn't going to be a slut or an old lady. There's a reason I didn't fight for sole custody. I didn't want her around all this shit."

"Not your decision," Torch said.

"A brand means you're tattooed," I said.

"Tattooed with what?" she asked.

"You're marked as property," Flicker said. "You can wear it on your arm or on your back. You'll also be given a cut that says you're property of the biker who claims you."

Ridley's brow furrowed. "I don't remember my mom having that."

Bull snorted. "Because I would have never made your mom my old lady. We were only together for a few days, then she came and found me when she discovered she was pregnant with you. But no matter what I think of your mother, I have always loved you. You're my sweet girl, and I hate to think of you living this life."

Ridley focused on him. "You taught me about bikes and introduced me to different MCs whenever you would visit. You never kept this way of life a secret from me, even if I don't know all the details. I don't need to know them. You're a good man, Daddy, and I'm sure you're not the only one in this room." Her gaze met mine. "I know you aren't. I've known Venom all my life, even if I wasn't around the last fourteen years. He would never hurt me."

Torch chuckled. "Are you laying claim to my VP?"

Her chin jutted up. "Maybe I am. Does that mean he has to get tattooed with *Property of Ridley*?"

Every man around the table roared with laughter, and even my lips twitched up in a smile. Girl had guts, I'd give her that.

"What about it, Venom?" Torch asked, humor shining in his eyes. "You going to get a *Property of Ridley* tattoo?"

My gaze scanned her from head to toe before flicking back up to her eyes. So, my baby girl thought to claim me? I scooted my chair back and crooked my finger at her. Ridley glared at Tank's hand still gripping her arm and tore it free before walking over to me. I reached for her waist and lifted her onto my lap, her legs splayed on either side of me as her hands went to my shoulders.

Her body trembled, and the need in her eyes made me want to bury my cock deep in her pussy and never come out. But before I claimed her, I needed to make sure she understood what she was getting into. It was one thing to joke about it, but quite another to make her mine.

"Baby girl, all kidding aside, we're not talking about something temporary. If I claim you, it's forever. You don't walk away. You get pissed at me, we deal with it. I hurt your feelings, you tell me. But once you're mine, your ass better be in my bed every fucking night. You'll do what I say, when I say, because sometimes it might mean the difference between life and death. It will be my job to protect you, even if you don't agree with my methods."

"If I'm in your bed every night, does that mean you're only with me?" she asked so softly I almost didn't hear.

"Are you asking me to be faithful?"

She nodded slowly. "It would break my heart if you were to ever be with someone else. I'd rather not have you at all than only have part of you."

She was fucking killing me.

"If I'm yours," she said. "I want you to be mine too."

Oh, baby girl. I already am.

My gaze held steady on hers, searching for any sign her feelings might waver. Her blue eyes were guileless, and seemed to promise me forever. I tore my gaze from hers and looked at Torch.

"Call Zipper," I said. "If Ridley's mom or anyone else tries to take her from me, I'll rain down hell on them. I want her marked now so every fucker out there knows she's mine."

Torch smiled and nodded.

Bull pushed his chair back and glared at me. "I can't stop you from claiming her. Anyone else, I'd have kicked their ass, but you're my VP. I'm going to give you the benefit of the doubt. But you disrespect her, fuck around on her, or break her damn heart, and I will gut you like a fucking fish."

"I will protect her with my life," I promised Bull. "And if I ever break her heart, I'm sure she'll kick my ass before you get a chance."

Bull grudgingly smiled. "You might be right about that. I might not have been able to spend much time with her, but I made sure my girl was tough and not some rotten-ass socialite who cried over a broken nail."

I looked away from Bull and reached up to fist Ridley's hair. Dragging her face closer to mine, I kissed her hard and deep, my tongue thrusting between her lips so she'd have no doubt who she belonged to. From this moment on, she was mine. I'd brand her, not only with ink and a cut, but I'd fucking brand her with my cum. I was going to fuck her until there was no doubt she was the property of Venom.

Chapter Five

Ridley

Zipper had a room at the back of the clubhouse with a chair and everything else he'd need. I'd decided to get the brand on my arm, even though Venom had whispered in my ear how much he'd love to pound my pussy from behind while seeing his name on my skin. That was one fantasy he'd have to give up because I was deathly afraid of needles, so the smaller the tattoo the better. Maybe I could custom order some temporary tattoos so he could get what he wanted without me being in a world of pain.

I sat on the leather chair, my body tense as Zipper rolled around the room on his stool, gathering everything he'd need. He'd explained the process to me and already gone over aftercare, but my nerves were shot. I wanted to be Venom's, and I'd go through with this for him, but I was so damn scared.

Venom stood on my other side, holding my hand. He gave it a squeeze and winked at me. I wondered if he could feel how badly I was shaking. There was a knock on the door, and Zipper rolled over to open it. The Prospect who'd been tending bar stepped inside and handed me a shot glass full of amber liquid.

"It will help," Venom said.

"As a licensed tattoo artist, I can't condone alcohol prior to a tattoo. Too much can mess with the ink," Zipper said. "But as a club member, take the shot. Maybe one will be enough to calm you down."

I grabbed the shot glass and tossed it back. The liquid burned my throat and made my eyes water. I coughed and sputtered before handing the glass back. The Prospect left, closing the door behind him. Zipper had set out a cup of black ink as well as a yellow and teal one. Venom had pulled him into the hall when Zipper had first arrived to tell him what he wanted, but I was completely in the dark. Since it was going on my body, it would have been nice if they'd shared the plan with me.

Zipper picked up the tattoo gun in his gloved hand and turned to face me. "You ready?"

"If I say no, can we just pretend I got the tattoo?"

He chuckled and shook his head. "Doesn't work that way."

"Then I guess I'm ready."

Venom held my hand a little tighter, letting me know that he was still there. I wanted to crawl into his lap and bury my face against his chest, but that hadn't been offered as an option. The gun buzzed to life, and I forced myself to remain still and tried to calm my racing heart. The first touch of the needle against my lower arm felt like fire was licking at my skin. I winced and looked away.

"It will be over soon enough, baby girl," Venom said.

Not soon enough in my opinion, but I'd agreed to be claimed by him, to live in his world, and I didn't think my opinion mattered that much anymore. The fact I was being labeled as property told me enough. Venom had warned me I'd have to do what he said when he said to do it, but I trusted him. He'd never tell me to do something that would put me in harm's way. And while I wasn't thrilled with getting a tattoo, it wasn't quite as horrible as I'd thought. The buzzing gun moved across my skin, and as the minutes ticked by, it hurt a little less. Or maybe I was just becoming numb to the pain.

My tattoo took not quite an hour, and when Zipper was finished, I finally looked down at my arm. In a pretty black script, it said *Property of Venom*. But there was a golden halo that dipped down over the word property and a set of teal angel wings that spread out to the sides of the words. The detail work on the feathers was incredible, but I looked up at him in confusion.

"Always thought you were a little angel," Venom said. "Even after all this time, your innocence and goodness shine from within. I imagine I'll get you a little dirty along the way, but you'll always be an angel in my eyes."

I pulled him down for a kiss, my lips gently brushing across his. Then Zipper was tugging my arm back down so he could put some sort of ointment on it and wrap it with Saran wrap. I probably should have paid closer attention so I'd know exactly what he was doing and why, but Venom had enough ink that I knew he'd take care of me.

"What now?" I asked as I rose to my feet.

Zipper smirked. "Now your man fights the urge to toss you over his shoulder and carry you back to his cave because I have no doubt everyone's waiting to celebrate. And you can't walk out on a celebration that's meant for you. You're not just Bull's daughter anymore, now you're Venom's old lady. And when the VP takes an old lady, the liquor will flow like honey."

"Doesn't it always?" I asked.

Zipper gave a bark of laughter. "I like her."

I gripped Venom's hand and let him lead me down the hallway and back to the bar. Music was blasting from a jukebox in the corner of the room, and bikers were sprawled in chairs with club sluts in their laps, or sitting on barstools getting shitfaced. My cheeks burned when I saw one of the girls sucking someone off right out in the open. I'd never seen this side of club life before, and I wondered if it would get wilder before the night was over.

Venom led me to a table in the corner where Tank and Flicker were sitting. I scanned the room, but didn't see my dad anywhere. I really didn't want to think about what he might be doing. The words "dad" and "sex" should never be put together in my mind, but it was likely he'd taken a woman back to his room. Wasn't that what the Prospect had said he was doing when I arrived?

Venom sat, his legs stretched in front of him, and he pulled me down onto his lap. His arm curled around my waist, and he kissed the side of my neck. The brother getting sucked off was seated at the next table, and I could hear the woman slurping on his cock. It didn't seem to bother anyone else, but I was a little uncomfortable. Was that what Venom was used to? I'd never even had sex before, much less done something in public.

I tipped my head back to whisper in his ear. "I know I said I'd do anything you told me to, but you aren't going to expect sexual favors in a public setting, are you?"

His arm tightened around me. "I wouldn't disrespect you that way, Ridley. You're my woman, not a whore. And you sure as shit won't be undressing in front of anyone. Any of these fuckers lay eyes on your bare skin and I'll have to put them in the fucking hospital."

His words made me feel a little better, even if the woman one table over was still making me uncomfortable. From the corner of my eye, I saw the biker grab her head and force his cock down her throat.

When he was finished, he zipped up and sent her on her way. It baffled me why a woman would agree to that kind of life. Sure, I'd agreed to be claimed by Venom, but that woman had no sooner sucked off one biker than another had her unfastening his pants. Why would someone agree to be passed around like that?

My confusion and revulsion must have shown on my face. Venom leaned in closer, his lips brushing my ear. "Those girls are hoping to become old ladies, thinking one of us will fall under their spell. They're here for entertainment and spread their legs for whoever wants them. No isn't a word they're allowed to use, and they're used every night by multiple brothers. Sometimes at the same time."

"And you enjoyed that?" I asked softly.

He chuckled. "When I was younger and didn't know better. When I became a Prospect, I did what all the guys did. Didn't take me long to realize I didn't want someone who had been passed around all night." His nose traced the shell of my ear. "Which means you're fucking perfect because no one's ever touched you but me. And no one ever will. You're mine, baby girl. I'm going to drive my cock into your tight little pussy and take that innocence you've held onto for so long."

His words made my thighs clench as moisture slicked my pussy. I knew it was only a matter of time, that once we left the clubhouse, he'd take me home and claim me. I'd already experienced pleasure in his arms, but I wanted to feel his cock inside me. The thought of him driving into me, claiming me, gave me a thrill. I loved it when he talked all rough and dirty.

Venom nipped my ear. "Did that turn you on, baby? You like it when I talk about fucking your little pussy, don't you? I bet you want me to take you hard and deep. I'm going to stretch you wide and fill you with my cum, because there will never be a barrier between us. I'm taking you raw, baby girl. I've never gone in bare before and I can't fucking wait to feel those slick little lips of yours around my dick. You're so fucking tight you're going to pull the cum from my balls."

I bit my lip to stifle my moan and squirmed on his lap. Venom kissed my neck again, and adjusted his hold so that his hand was cupping the underside of my breast. My nipples hardened, and I wondered how long we had to be sociable. I ached for him. He'd given me multiple orgasms with his mouth and hands, but I wanted more. I wanted to experience everything with Venom. As long as nothing he asked of me hurt, I was willing to try anything with him. I might be inexperienced, but I was eager to learn. I wanted to please him, wanted him to want me with the same hunger I felt for him.

Venom talked quietly to Tank and Flicker, the three of them tossing back shots. I didn't understand half of what they were saying, since it was all club related, so I used my time to study my surroundings. The bikers were a rowdy lot, and apparently a lusty one. Some led the girls back to their rooms, others just fucked them right out in the open. More than one woman was completely naked as they strolled around the clubhouse. I felt a little like I'd fallen down the rabbit hole.

I didn't see any women except the club sluts, and I wondered if there were other old ladies. I thought I remembered some women and children being around when I was younger. Maybe they were smart enough to stay away from all this. I could now understand why my dad had said he didn't want this life for me. If this is what happened every night, I didn't think I wanted to be a part of it. And yet, if I stayed home and Venom came alone, what was to stop one of those whores from crawling all over him? He'd promised to be faithful, but it didn't mean they wouldn't try to tempt him.

There didn't seem to be a short supply of alcohol, and I lost track of how many drinks Venom had thrown back. His hands began to wander as he talked to his brothers. When he slid his hand between my legs, I "accidentally" jabbed him with my elbow. I had no problem with him touching me, actually craved his touch, but not here. Not like this. His hand cupped me, and he gave me a squeeze. My cheeks flushed hotly, and I jumped up.

"Where the fuck are you going?" Venom asked. The glassiness of his eyes told me he'd had way too much to drink.

"I'm going home. I need to take care of my tattoo and I'd like a shower."

His eyes narrowed. "Home?"

"Yeah, you know that place where we spent most of the day? It's been a long day, Venom. I just want to go home, clean up, and rest for a bit. I was on the road for about ten hours last night and into this morning."

His gaze softened and he nodded. "I'll take you home, baby girl."

He tossed back another shot before rising to his feet. I watched him warily, wondering just how drunk he was, but his walk was steady and he didn't stumble or stagger even once. It probably wasn't smart getting on the back of his bike when he'd been drinking, though. I reached out to place my hand on his arm, pulling him to a stop.

"Thought you wanted to go home," he said.

"I do, but you've been drinking all night." I bit my lip, not sure if I was about to overstep, or what the repercussions would be if I did.

"Are you saying I'm drunk?" His eyes flashed with anger.

"I just... I don't want either of us to get hurt on the way home. What if your reflexes are a little slower than usual? You've been throwing back shots for about an hour now."

Venom grabbed my arm and lifted it. "See this? It means I tell you what to do, not the other way around."

Tears pricked my eyes, but I refused to let them fall. This wasn't the Venom who had wanted to protect me. That Venom wouldn't have taken a chance with my safety. He stared at me for the longest time before cursing under his breath. He took my hand and led me over to the bar, picking me up and setting me down on one of the stools. Venom sat next to me and motioned for the Prospect to come over.

"Get me some coffee," Venom said.

I didn't say anything, not sure how he'd take it.

The Prospect set a full mug in front of Venom, and my sexy biker took a big gulp. When he set the cup down, he stared into it before taking another swallow. When he finished that cup, he motioned for another. After the second cup, he left me at the bar long enough to use the bathroom, then came back to yet another full cup. By the time he'd finished his fourth cup of coffee, and almost an hour had passed, his eyes weren't as glassy as before. His gaze turned to me, and I saw remorse.

Venom reached up and cupped my cheek. "I'm sorry, baby girl. I can sometimes get nasty when I drink too much. It's never mattered before now."

"I didn't want to make you mad, but I was worried."

"Come here." He reached over and pulled me onto his lap, his arms going around me. "I promised to protect you, and I can't very well do that if I'm the one hurting you. Keeping you safe is my top priority, Ridley. I'll watch how much I drink when you're with me, so I won't scare you again. And I sure as fuck don't want to take a chance with your life and drive drunk. I've never had an accident, but if something were to happen, it would destroy me."

"Can we go home?" I asked softly. "I know this is all part of your world, but I think it's a little much for me. I like what we do in the bedroom, but to me it's private and should remain behind closed doors. Seeing everyone out in the open like this… "

Venom kissed me. "I understand. None of the old ladies hang out in the clubhouse unless it's a family day. I shouldn't have asked you to stay. Not really sure I like you seeing anyone's dick other than mine anyway."

A faint smile traced my lips. "Well, I saw plenty of them tonight."

He growled softly and then kissed me harder. "That shit's not gonna happen again. Fuckers better stay zipped when you're around. No reason they can't take the whores to their rooms."

"Take me home and make me yours," I said softly. "Your cock is the only one I'm interested in."

"Damn well better be."

I slid off his lap and tugged on his hand. "Let's go home."

"You aren't really tired, are you?" he asked. "I know you said you wanted to rest."

"You could probably talk me into staying awake for a while."

Venom leaned in close. "For a while? Baby girl, I'm going to fuck you all night long. My cock has been aching to be inside you, and while those sweet lips of yours were pretty amazing, and I sure as hell liked coming down your throat, I want to feel that tight pussy squeezing me."

His words made my breath quicken and my heart race. In the darkness outside the clubhouse, he cupped me through my jeans and rubbed his cock against my ass. His lips traced the curve of my neck, his whiskers tickling me.

"If we were alone, I'd take you right here, right now," he murmured. His hand slid up and he popped the button on my jeans, eased my zipper down, and his hand slipped inside my panties. His fingers stroked my pussy, and my legs nearly gave out. "So fucking wet. You want my cock bad, don't you, baby girl?"

"Yes," I moaned. "So bad."

"Maybe I should take the edge off."

My eyes scanned the darkness, but everyone was inside except the Prospect at the gate, and he was too far away to see us. Two of Venom's fingers slid inside my channel, pumping in and out. The heel of his hand ground against my clit.

"Venom," I whispered.

"Mine." His fingers stroked faster. "This sopping wet pussy is all mine, and I'm going to fuck it good and hard when I get you home. But first you're going to take my cock in your mouth and suck me dry, because I want you so fucking bad that I'll blow the second this tight pussy squeezes my dick."

I panted and tried to remain upright.

"You like sucking my cock, don't you, baby girl?"

"Yes."

"Say it."

"I like sucking your cock. I like it when you come in my mouth."

He growled, and his fingers fucked me faster until I was biting my tongue to hold back my cries of pleasure. I came so hard I nearly saw stars, and still his fingers stroked me. I sagged against him as his hand slipped out of my pants, and he fastened my jeans again.

"Come on, baby girl. I have plans for you tonight."

Wordlessly, I followed him to his bike and climbed on behind him. My arms went around his waist, and I held on tight as the engine roared to life. The tires spit gravel as Venom took off toward home, riding like the devil himself was after us. My pussy was still sensitive from coming so hard, and the vibration from the bike was nearly enough to make me come again. My thighs squeezed tighter around Venom, and I could have sworn I heard him laugh. I had no doubt he'd ease this endless ache. My hand drifted down his abdomen and teased the length of him through his jeans. His laughter turned to a groan, and with a twist of the throttle, the bike shot forward even faster than before.

It seemed I wasn't the only one who had an ache that needed easing.

Chapter Six

Venom

The thrum of my bike between my legs and the wind on my face cleared the rest of the alcohol from my system as we sped down the road toward my house. Ridley was glued to my back, her thighs squeezing my hips, and those wandering fucking hands of hers… One more stroke of her fingers against my cock, and I was going to come in my pants like a horny teenager. She better be damn glad she wasn't wearing a skirt or I'd have pulled over, hauled her around in front of me, and fucked her on the bike. That was definitely a fantasy we were going to play out later.

I pulled the bike into the driveway and killed the engine. I felt a tremor run through Ridley before she swung her leg over the back and got off. Removing the keys from the ignition, I grabbed her hand and led her up to the front door. The anticipation shining in her eyes had me fumbling with the damn keys. I dropped them twice before finding the one for the house. The door no sooner swung open than I dragged her inside, slamming it shut and twisting the lock into place.

Ridley launched herself at me, slamming my back against the door, as her lips fused to mine. Her tongue thrust into my mouth as her hands worked my belt loose, then unzipped my jeans and shoved them down my thighs. She stroked my cock, spreading the pre-cum over the head and down my shaft. She felt so fucking good I couldn't help but thrust into her small hand. I wasn't about to come all over her fingers, though.

I gripped her hair and pulled her away from my lips, tugging her down to her knees. "Open up, baby girl."

Her jaw dropped and she worked my cock into her mouth, tipping her head back like I'd shown her before. Fuck but she felt good! I thrust in and out of her hot, wet mouth, my dick going deeper with every stroke until she was taking all of me. Pleasure rolled over me, and I didn't dare close my fucking eyes. I wanted to watch as I fucked her mouth. She hummed as I filled her mouth again, and damn if I almost didn't come. I knew I was close, but I wasn't ready yet. I loved having her mouth on me and wanted to enjoy it a little longer.

"That's it, baby. Take all of it. Your mouth is fucking incredible."

I thrust harder, faster. Plunging deep I came so hard I nearly stopped breathing. Pulling out of her mouth, I sagged against the door a moment. I dragged my jeans up to my hips, then tossed Ridley over my shoulder and went straight to the bedroom. I let her drop to the bed with a bounce and began shrugging out of my cut. She scrambled to her feet and was undressed before I'd even pulled off my boots and jeans.

She was so damn perfect. Looking at her soft curves and creamy skin was quickly becoming my favorite thing to do. Well, aside from fucking her. I had no doubt that once I got inside her, I'd never want to come back out. I'd felt how fucking tight her pussy was, and I couldn't wait to feel it wrapped around my cock. She was mine. Only mine. No one had sucked those pretty pink nipples except me. No one had tongue-fucked her until she screamed their name, except me. And no cock had ever entered her pussy, and none ever would except mine. I already felt so damn possessive of her, wanted to own every fucking inch of her. I could tell I was going to be a jealous asshole when it came to Ridley.

My fingers skimmed over her cheek, down her neck, and didn't stop until I was cupping her breast. Her nipple hardened against my palm, and I stroked it. I cupped her other breast with my other hand, caressing and squeezing the mounds, until Ridley was breathing harder and her skin was flushed. I knew this first time would hurt, and I wanted her so ready for me that the pain would be minimal. I'd never been with a virgin before, not even when I was one, but the guys around the clubhouse talked. Several had popped the cherries of some random girls. They said it was the best feeling in the world, except for taking a tight virgin ass.

Leaning down, I took her nipple in my mouth, sucking hard on the tip. My teeth lightly scraped it before switching to the other side. Her hands slid into my hair as I licked, sucked, and nipped one nipple, then the other, going back and forth until her breasts were pink with whisker burn.

"Sit on the edge of the bed, baby girl. Lean back on your elbows and spread those pretty thighs. Show me that gorgeous pussy."

Her eyes darkened with desire as she did as I'd commanded. Her thighs parted, and the lips of her pussy slowly spread open. She was already slick and ready for me, but I wasn't going to take her yet. It might fucking kill me, but she was going to scream my name and beg for my cock before I gave it to her. But first, I was going to admire the view. I slid my fingers down her slick lips before plunging two inside her. I loved watching her pussy grip the digits tight, sucking them in. Her pussy was hungry, and I could tell it was greedy for my cock.

Her cream coated my fingers as I stroked them in and out of her. Ridley moaned and closed her eyes, her cheeks flushing.

"Open your eyes, baby girl. You better be looking at me when you come."

Her eyes snapped open, and her gaze found mine. Lowering to my knees, I withdrew my fingers and replaced them with my mouth. She tasted so fucking good. I devoured her soft, pink flesh, sliding my tongue into her tight channel. I groaned and thrust my tongue into her again, flicking it in and out. My hands gripped her thighs, pushing them wide. Her pussy was open and eager for my mouth. My gaze held hers as I ate her until she screamed. I felt the gush of her release against my face and kept licking until she was trembling.

"Please, Venom," she begged softly.

"Please what, baby girl? Tell me what you want."

"I want to feel you inside me."

My tongue plunged inside her again.

"N-no. Your cock."

I stood and wiped off my face. My hands gripped her hips, lifting her ass off the bed. I thrust my cock along the seam of her pussy, coating it in her cream. She moaned and opened wider for me. The head of my cock pressed against her small opening, and I slowly pushed inside. It took shallow thrusts to work myself into her tight channel. Only half my dick was inside her when I felt her tense.

"Easy, baby girl. It's only going to hurt for a minute." I hoped like hell I wasn't lying.

With one deep thrust, I went balls deep inside her. Ridley let out a scream that I wouldn't soon forget, and tears slipped down her cheeks. She was so fucking tight and felt so good that I had to grind my teeth to keep from taking her as hard and deep as possible. I wanted to pound into her pussy until my balls emptied, and then I wanted to keep fucking her. Slowly, she began to relax.

"I think you can move now," she said.

I pulled my hips back and slid in deep again. This time there wasn't pain in her eyes. I watched as my dick tunneled in and out of her, streaks of her blood coating my shaft. I'd never seen a prettier sight than her pussy gripping me tight. Fucking Ridley had just become my favorite thing to do. I drove in harder, and fuck if she didn't take every inch of my cock like she was born for it.

"Watch us, baby girl. We fit together so perfectly."

She leaned up and watched my dick slide in and out of her. I felt my cock swell and knew I was close to coming. Reaching for her clit, I stroked it with my thumb. I'd be damned if I was going to finish before her. I kept my thrusts steady as I rubbed her clit in small, tight circles. When she came, my name on her lips, and pussy squeezing me, I couldn't hold back. I held her hips in both hands as I fucked her like a man possessed. Hard. Deep. A growl left me as my cum bathed the inside of her. I didn't stop thrusting until every last drop had been drained from my balls.

I refused to let her go, didn't pull my cock out. Even though I'd come, I was still hard for her. I knew she'd be sore tomorrow, but after I left her rest a few minutes, I started fucking her again. Her eyes went wide with the first stroke, as if she couldn't believe I was ready to go again. Hell, I could hardly believe it. Her cum and mine had mingled and eased the way.

She was still tight as fuck, but I slid inside her with little effort.

I pulled out and watched as our fluids slipped from her pussy, then pushed back in. I'd marked her as mine in every way possible. She wore my brand on her skin, would soon wear my cut, and now she wore my cum. I wanted to pump her so full of it that she would still be dripping tomorrow.

"Am I hurting you?" I asked, pausing.

She shook her head and bit her lip.

"Think you can come again?" I asked.

"I want to."

"Play with that pussy, baby girl. Stroke that hard little clit until you're milking my cock dry."

Her hand slid down her belly, and her fingers slipped between the lips of her pussy to rub herself. My gaze was hungry as I watched her fingers dance across that little bud, and I fucked her harder. It wasn't long before she was coming again, her pussy rippling along my cock. I pounded her sweet pussy, driving my cock into her again and again until my cum erupted from my cock and filled her up.

As I pulled out of her, my cum trickled out. I used my fingers to shove it back inside her, stroking her a few times. Her pussy was swollen and pink. Leaning down, I pressed my lips to the slick lips and groaned at our combined scents. I couldn't resist a taste and my tongue flicked out. Ridley gasped and tried to close her thighs, but only ended up holding my head in place. I chuckled and licked her one more time before pulling away.

"I'm going to run a bath for you, baby girl. A nice soak in some hot water will keep you from being quite so sore."

"Will you join me in the tub?" she asked.

"If that's what you want."

"I'll always want you with me, Venom. I'm yours, and you're mine." Her eyes narrowed. "And if any of those club sluts so much as touch you, I'll break their hands."

My lips twitched with humor. Now that she was officially mine, if she said that shit in front of my brothers, I'd have had to correct her. Otherwise, they'd think my woman ruled this relationship, and that shit wouldn't do for the VP of the motherfucking club. But here in our home, I liked seeing this side of her. I got a secret thrill that she was jealous about other women touching me. She didn't have a damn thing to worry about, though. The only woman I wanted was her. Now that my dick had gotten a taste of her, no other pussy would ever do. There wasn't one out there as tight or as sweet as hers. My gaze fastened between her legs again, and my cock started getting hard. Before I did something stupid, like take her again, I walked into the bathroom and started the water.

I didn't have any of that scented crap women liked, so I hoped she wouldn't mind just plain water. When the tub was full, I shut off the taps and went to get Ridley. Her eyes were closed, but slowly opened when I neared the bed. She gave me a drowsy smile, and I felt like an ass for keeping her awake so long. Lifting her into my arms, I carried her into the bathroom and stepped into the tub. I released her long enough to sit down, then she settled in front of me, her back pressed to my chest.

My hand caressed her stomach, and I wondered if we'd already made a baby. Everything had happened so fast with us that we hadn't even discussed kids. Since she'd never been with anyone before, I doubted she was on birth control. It was a little late now, but it was a conversation we should probably have sooner or later. This day had been long enough already, though, and I could feel the exhaustion in her heavy limbs. Or I could just knock her up. I liked the thought of her round with my child. My hand slipped between her legs, and I gently rubbed her pussy. She was still swollen, and I hoped I hadn't been too rough with her. The last thing I ever wanted to do was hurt Ridley.

I wrapped an arm around her waist and kissed the top of her head. Ridley murmured something and I smiled. She was already falling back asleep. I held her in the hot water a few more minutes, knowing that a good soak would be the best thing for her, then I carried her back to the bedroom, not caring that she got the bedding wet. After draining the tub and drying off, I crawled into bed beside her. She immediately sought me out, cuddling against my side.

Holding my woman close, I closed my eyes and breathed deep. The room smelled like sex, but Ridley's soft scent was just under that. If anyone had told me I'd have an old lady, I'd have laughed at them. Pussy had always come easy to me, but knowing Ridley was mine was the best feeling in the world. Yeah, she was probably too fucking young for me, but I wasn't letting her go. The moment she'd looked into my eyes, she'd been mine.

I just hoped I never gave her cause to regret her decision to be with me. I could be an outright bastard, had done some really fucked up shit, but Ridley lit up my dark world. I'd never think twice about laying my life down for her. Being with me might not be all rainbows and sunshine, and maybe she could have done better than a dirty old biker, but I'd make her my entire fucking world. What I felt for her was stronger than anything I'd experienced before. It was all consuming, and I knew I'd fuck up anyone who tried to come between us.

I might not be able to give her sweet words, but maybe what I could offer her would be enough. It would have to be. Love had never been part of my life, and I wouldn't have known the emotion if it bit me on the ass. But Ridley was mine, in every way, and the urge I had to possess every inch of her, to protect her and care for her, was stronger than some stupid word that people threw out carelessly.

"Mine," I said with a soft growl, my arm tightening around her. If she didn't know what she'd gotten herself into by accepting my brand, she would soon enough. Once something was mine, I never let it go. And Ridley was more than just mine. She was as essential as the air I breathed. I'd fucking die if she were gone.

One look. One fucking look. That's all it had taken.

Those gorgeous blue eyes of hers had met mine and I'd been gone for her.

Angels were damn near impossible to find, and now I'd have one in my arms the rest of my life.

I was a lucky fucking bastard and I knew it.

I just hoped that luck held out.

My phone buzzed in the pocket of my jeans. After last time, I wasn't about to ignore the call. I pulled away from Ridley, careful not to wake her, and grabbed my phone from the denim on the floor.

"What?" I asked when I answered the call.

"It's Wire. We need to fucking talk."

"So talk."

"This isn't the kind of shit you say over the phone."

I glanced at Ridley. "My woman just went to sleep. It's been a long-ass day, and she needs some rest. I can't leave her here unprotected."

"Fine. Sleep a few hours, then get your asses to the clubhouse. It's probably better if she hears this too. You have no idea what kind of miracle it is she made it here."

Dread settled in my gut, and I knew that whatever Wire told us was going to change things. I ended the call and crawled back into bed with Ridley, but fuck me if sleep would come. There were too many monsters lurking in the dark, and for the first time in forever, I wondered if there was something bigger and badder than me out there.

Chapter Seven

Ridley

Wire's room at the clubhouse was different from Venom's. This one still had a bed and dresser, but it was easily twice the size and had a bank of monitors and computer equipment. Despite the fact the biker seemed very tech savvy, and was apparently some sort of hacker, geeky wasn't the word I'd use to describe him. His ginger hair and green eyes made him look a little less hardcore than the other bikers, and his face was open and friendly when he looked at me. But the man was packing muscle, and when he started talking about my stepdad and Montoya, there was a hardness that entered his eyes. Whoever Wire was, he had earned the patches on his cut, and if anyone stepped into a dark alley with him, I had no doubt they wouldn't make it out the other side.

"Ridley, what I have to say, and the things you might see, are going to upset you. If Venom wants you to leave, I would understand, but I think you need to know what kind of people you're dealing with. We're going to protect you, but I won't lie. We're walking a dangerous line," Wire said.

"What do you mean the things she might see?" Venom asked, his hand tight on mine.

Wire looked at me. "Did you know that your stepdad had cameras set up around his house?"

I shrugged. "He mentioned something about a security system. Is it part of that?"

"Maybe the lower level is, but there were cameras in your bedroom and bathroom."

My breath caught and my eyes widened. "Why would he have cameras there?"

"Because he was spying on you. And he recorded and kept quite a bit of the footage." Wire looked fucking pissed when he turned his gaze to Venom. "It's bad, man. The recordings go back to when she was about thirteen years old. And a lot of it has her naked on camera."

Venom growled, and his face flushed with anger. "That sick fucking bastard. If I get my hands on him, I'll rip off his goddamn balls."

"There's more," Wire said. "Like I said, some of the videos go back to a time when Ridley looks to be about thirteen, but the older she got the more video clips there were. This may be embarrassing for you, Ridley. Are you sure you want to see this?"

"I need to know," I said softly.

Wire nodded and turned to his computers, hitting a few keystrokes. A video popped up on the large monitor of my bedroom at my stepdad's mansion. I was lying naked on my bed, my legs spread and my fingers rubbing my pussy. I gasped and my face flushed. The video switched angles partway through, and you could see in detail what I was doing. I felt so sick I thought I might throw up. Venom was breathing hard, and his body shook with fury.

"Do you know when this was taken, Ridley?" Wire asked.

I shook my head, but then focused more on the room in the video. The poster on one wall was no longer hanging in that room and hadn't been for at least two years.

"I think I was seventeen, maybe sixteen."

"And this one?" Wire asked, switching to a video of me in the shower. I was not only washing my body, but it was another clip of me pleasuring myself. My pussy was bare in this one, which meant it was more recent.

"That had to have been taken in the last year."

"Who's seen these?" Venom asked.

"Out of the MC? Just you and me. And I won't ever let another fucking soul see them, unless I'm ordered to do so. But I pulled these from Benton's emails. When I finished with his financials, I dug deeper and hacked into his personal and work email accounts. These videos, a total of about a dozen spanning what looks like six years, were sent to Montoya over the last eight months."

"He was planning to sell me to that monster all this time?" I asked.

"I'm afraid this is just the tip of the iceberg," Wire said. "I used some special software I have to scour the internet, and I dug fucking deep, to see if these videos were posted anywhere else. Montoya apparently has a site where he auctions off time with his girls. He has a full stable in a range of ages, sizes, and colors. Some of Ridley's videos are on that site and bidding has already begun. He's promised them that she'll be well broken in when they get her."

"Show me," Venom said.

Wire hesitated only a moment before giving a nod and pulling up the site. I couldn't hold back anymore. I ran for the trash can by the door and threw up several times. Some of the girls on the front page hadn't even hit puberty yet. How was it a monster like that was out wandering the streets? Venom rubbed my back and pulled me into his arms.

I glanced at the screen again, this time it was my page that was loaded. The words on the screen made me ill again. He'd offered to let the men do whatever they wanted to me, as long as I was returned without scarring. Some of the bids on the screen were from men in groups of three or more, their comments making bile rise in my throat and I ended up puking again.

"How do you want to handle this?" Wire asked. "I can disable this page, but as long as he has a copy of the videos, he can just put another one up. Even if I trace this IP address and hack his system, there's no guarantee he doesn't have a backup somewhere. As much money as he's making off these girls, I'd imagine he has several backups."

"Why did my stepdad and mom do this to me?" I asked.

"That big house and those fancy cars? He's about to lose them all. Benton made some bad investments and he's not only broke, but some unsavory people will be asking for their money soon. The cash he gets from Montoya for you won't make him rich again, but it will keep him alive," Wire said.

"Oh, he's fucking dead already," Venom said. "Send a crew to fetch Mr. and Mrs. Richard Benton III and bring them here. I'd like to have a little chat with them."

"What do we do about Montoya?" Wire asked.

"Can you find out where that site is based?" Venom asked. "As much as I'd love to get my hands on the fucker and bury him six feet deep, that would bring all kinds of shit to our doorstep. A man like that is going to be too damn well-connected."

Wire's eyes narrowed. "What are you thinking?"

"I'm thinking if that's a US-based site, the Feds might like to know he's selling young girls to the highest bidder. More than one of those videos of Ridley are from when she was just a kid. That should earn him some hard time behind bars, for a really fucking long time," Venom said.

"What are you going to do with my mom and stepdad?" I asked.

Venom's eyes were cold when he looked down at me. "You don't want to know."

I stared up at him and waited to feel some sort of emotion over the fact he was likely going to kill my mother, but whatever love I'd once had for her was long gone. I reached up and cupped his cheek, his whiskers tickling my fingers.

"Do whatever you have to do. I trust you," I told him

Venom grasped my hand and pressed a kiss to my palm.

"I'll make copies of everything," Wire said. "But when the Feds see Benton's name attached to some of the images on Montoya's site, they're going to go looking for him."

"So make it look like he skipped town and hopped a flight to a non-extradition country, taking his bitch-ass whore of a wife with him." Venom's lips thinned in a grim line. "I want them. They're going to pay for what they've done to Ridley. They may not have succeeded in handing her off to Montoya, because my girl is tough as nails and got the fuck out of there, but those sick fucks have been recording her during intimate moments for years. They were supposed to love her, protect her. Not sell her to the highest damn bidder."

"I'll arrange for a crew to pick up the Bentons and bring them here," Wire said. "I'll set up the paper trail for them leaving the country, and I'll make sure a copy of everything I've found is forwarded to the authorities. Anonymously, of course."

"Won't they be able to trace it back to you?" I asked.

Wire smiled. "Honey, if I don't want to be found, no one can find me."

Venom chuckled. "Wire did time from the age of ten to eighteen for not only hacking into our government files, but those of several other countries as well. At the time of his arrest, he was hailed as the top hacker in the country. Now he's probably the best in the damn world."

My eyes widened. "But if you got into that kind of trouble, can't you go back to jail for even looking at a computer?"

"The authorities aren't coming anywhere near the Dixie Reapers compound," Wire said. "Besides, I take an odd job here and there, help out big brother from time to time. They leave me alone, as long as I don't bring the entire system down."

"You can do that?"

Wire shrugged.

I'd never met anyone like him before, and while I'd known the gun on his hip made him dangerous, I was now certain that his computer skills were what made him possibly the deadliest man in the MC. To have that kind of power, and all at his fingertips... a few keystrokes and I wondered if he could wipe out an entire country. I was a little in awe.

"You said you needed to know what country Montoya's site was based in before turning the files over to anyone," I said.

"Won't hurt to send a copy to the Feds. You're an American, and you were underage in some of those videos. They'll be interested. I'll still track down where the site originated and send that info along too. If it's not based in our country, which I suspect it's not since Montoya is Columbian, the Feds can figure out the best way to handle things. Like Venom said, that man would bring more shit to our door than we're probably prepared to handle. We'll get justice for you, Ridley, it just might be done through legal channels instead of our more colorful way." Wire smiled. "I promise, they're all going to pay, in some way or another."

I nodded and took Venom's hand. "I think I've seen enough for today."

Venom tipped my chin up and leaned down, but I turned my head at the last second so that his lips brushed my cheek.

"You are so not kissing me after I've been puking."

He chuckled and led me out of Wire's room. His room was two doors down and he unlocked it and pulled me inside. "There's a toothbrush in the bathroom and some mouthwash. Use whatever you want."

"You don't mind me using your toothbrush?" I asked.

His eyebrow arched. "Baby girl, I've had my tongue in your mouth and my dick down your throat... and you think I'm going to mind you borrowing my toothbrush?"

My cheeks warmed. When he put it like that... I stepped into the small bathroom and brushed my teeth twice before rinsing liberally with mouthwash. My stomach wasn't quite as knotted up, but the thought of my stepdad and other men watching me do that made me ill. Those moments had been private, and I'd thought I was safely locked in my room, where no one could see me. I felt defiled all over again, and this was even worse than Montoya putting his hand on me. At least that had been one incident with one man, but how many thousands or millions of sick perverts had seen those videos online? And the things they'd posted... my stomach gurgled again, but I pressed a hand to my belly and took some deep breaths.

Venom was leaning against the wall when I went back into his bedroom, his arms folded over his massive chest. He studied me a moment before holding out a hand to me. I didn't hesitate even a second before folding myself against his big body. He made me feel safe, and if Venom said everything would be okay, then I knew it would be.

"I don't like the idea of you leaving the compound until we have all these loose ends tied up, but you couldn't have had much in that bag you brought with you," Venom said. "I'm going to get two of the Prospects and our Enforcer, then we're going shopping in town. It's going to be a quick trip, so just grab some essentials. The Prospects can take the truck, so buy as much shit as you want, just do it fast."

I nodded. I was down to one change of clothes and really did need more stuff.

"I don't have much money left," I admitted.

Venom growled before pressing his lips to mine. "My woman doesn't pay for her own shit. I told you, it's my job to take care of you. Anything you need, ever, you just tell me."

"All right," I agreed softly.

He kissed me again, harder and deeper, before dragging me out of his room. A smile teased my lips as I saw the hard ridge of his arousal. I had no doubt that if we had more time, he'd have stripped me and fucked me, even if we were in the clubhouse. The man was insatiable, but then, when it came to Venom, so was I. My pussy was still a little sore from last night, but I ached to feel him inside me again. I'd never felt closer to anyone than I did with Venom.

When we approached the bar, I noticed a black leather vest on the bar top. It was much smaller than Venom's, and the man sitting on the stool beside it tossed it to my man. Venom caught it with ease, then held it up. *Property of Venom -- Dixie Reapers MC VP* was stitched across the back along with the club logo. On the front were the same words but much smaller. Venom held it open, and I slipped my arms into it.

"Now there's no doubt you're my old lady," he said before nipping my ear. "I fucking love seeing my name on you. You leave the house, you wear this. Got it?"

I nodded.

"I don't care if you're wearing a damn dress. You don't wander around without this cut. It's not just words, Ridley. It means you're fucking mine and anyone who touches you is going to answer to me. It might seem like a harmless piece of leather with some stitching, but it's protection."

"I understand."

He pressed his lips to mine. "Come on, baby girl. Let's get you some new clothes, then I'm going to take you home."

I leaned into his hard body. "And just what are we going to do when we get home?"

His lips tickled my ear as he spoke low enough only I could hear him. "I'm going to strip you bare, then put that cut back on you, and I'm going to pound your fucking pussy from behind. I'm so fucking hard just thinking about seeing my name across your back while I take you. Going to fill you so full of my cum, baby girl, but once won't be enough. I'm going to fuck you until that pussy is all pink and swollen, then I'm going to kiss it all better so we can do it again."

I bit my lip to stifle the moan that sprang to my lips, and I practically dragged him out of the clubhouse. He chuckled and called out to three men over his shoulder as I pulled him down the steps and toward his bike. Using his body to shield me from prying eyes, Venom kissed me hungrily and reached up to tweak my nipple through my shirt. If he hadn't promised me new clothes, I'd have begged him to take me home. Already I ached for him and couldn't wait to get him alone. But common sense won out. Barely.

When we made it to town, Venom only left my side for a short while, leaving me in the care of Tank, the club's Enforcer, and the two Prospects.

"I have an errand to run, baby girl, but I'll be quick." His voice lowered. "And I promise it will be worth it."

I didn't have any idea what he was up to, but I suddenly couldn't wait to find out.

Chapter Eight

Venom

My girl's eyes had gone wide when she saw the little surprise I'd picked up in town the other day. While I'd thoroughly fucked her pussy and her mouth since claiming her, there was one thing I had yet to do with her. My dick was dying to get inside that tight ass of hers, but I knew if she wasn't properly prepared, with my size, it would hurt like fuck. So I'd bought a butt plug and a bottle of lube. I'd given her time to get used to the idea, but I was done waiting.

Ridley was sprawled on her stomach, the morning sun filtering through the blinds and highlighting her gorgeous curves. I dragged the sheet off her body and ran my hand over her ass. She didn't know it yet, but this was going to be mine today. I just had a little business to take care of first, and then the rest of the day I was hers.

I spread her ass cheeks and groaned at the sight of the tight little hole I so badly wanted to fuck. The toy and lube sat on the bedside table, where I'd left it since getting it from the store. I'd already opened the package and washed the rubber plug. My finger gently pressed against her small opening, and I massaged it. Ridley moaned in her sleep and thrust her ass back at me. I'd been playing back here a little the last few days, but not enough to stretch her for my dick.

I straddled her thighs and ran kisses down her spine, then nipped her butt cheek. Ridley gasped, and her eyes flew open.

"Morning, baby girl. Today's the day."

"What day?" she asked, her voice husky with sleep.

"Today's the day I'm going to fuck this ass. Remember what we talked about?"

She slowly nodded.

I reached for the lube and toy, then spread her cheeks wide while I drizzled the liquid onto her hole. It tightened, and my dick got so fucking hard I knew I'd have to fuck her before I left for the morning. I used my fingers to loosen her up a little, stroking and massaging until she was relaxing and letting me in farther. When I thought she was ready, I lubed the toy and slowly inserted it into her ass. The plug was just big enough to help ease my way, but nowhere near the size of my dick.

I leaned over Ridley and gently bit her shoulder. My hand slipped under her belly and lifted her ass in the air. "Going to fuck you, baby girl. It's going to be hard and it's going to be fast, but I have to fucking have you. So damn hard for you, baby."

I drew away from her and gripped her hips. Pulling her ass toward me, I lined my cock up and sank into her sweet pussy. I spread her ass cheeks wide while I pounded into her. Seeing the plug in her ass and knowing I would be taking her there later ignited something inside me. I took her like a demon possessed, pounding her tight little pussy until she was screaming out my name and begging for more. She'd no doubt be feeling my cock inside her for a while. I groaned as my cum shot out of my dick and slicked her channel, pumping furiously until every last drop had been drained from me. When I pulled out, I stared for a moment, admiring the puffy pink lips and the way our juices mingled and slid out of her.

If I didn't have business to take care of, I'd have stayed buried in her for hours. But I didn't have time to play anymore. I swatted her ass and went to get cleaned up. Ridley started to rise from the bed, and I gave her a stern look.

"What?" she asked.

"You keep my cum on you until I get back. And don't even think of taking that plug out of your ass. Every time you sit, I want you to think about what I'm going to do to you when I get home."

Her cheeks warmed, but I saw the desire in her eyes and knew that she wanted this every bit as much as I did, even if she wouldn't admit it out loud. I was going to take a shower, but decided against it. I didn't even bother cleaning up my dick, just pulled on my clothes, slipped on my boots and cut, and gave Ridley a kiss that would leave little doubt that she was my entire fucking world.

And now it was time to make sure she stayed safe.

As the engine of my bike roared to life, I stared up at the second floor of the house. My Ridley was up there, waiting for me to come back, and that was one of the best feelings in the world -- aside from being balls deep inside her because that was definitely my favorite. Watching the house a moment, I made myself a vow. Nothing like this nasty shit with her stepdad would ever touch her again. If the Feds didn't take down Montoya, I'd do whatever was necessary to put the fucker in the ground, and damn the consequences. Even if it rained hellfire down on my club, it would be worth it to give Ridley peace of mind.

I backed my bike down the driveway and took the road at breakneck speed. I bypassed the clubhouse and kept going until I reached my destination. The barn at the back of the property was so isolated on all sides, that no one would hear the screams of anyone inside. Bull and Tank were already inside, waiting on me to pass judgment on those who awaited punishment.

I stepped into the dimly lit interior, and the smell of piss reached my nose. Ridley's mom and stepass were tied to two chairs in the middle of the structure, their mouths gagged and their eyes blindfolded. Bull looked ready to tear into them, but now that Ridley was my old lady, he knew it would be me who brought justice for the girl we both cared for. I nodded at Tank, and he removed their gags and uncovered their eyes.

"Scream all you want, fuckers," Tank said. "No one will hear you."

"Whatever you want, you can have it," Benton said.

I folded my arms over my chest. "Really? How are you going to manage that when you're broke?"

"I'll be coming into some money soon," the asshat said.

"Do you even know where the fuck you are?" I asked.

Ridley's mom was looking at Bull, her face pale as she realized the seriousness of their situation.

"Shut the fuck up, Richard," she said.

It seemed the stepass didn't know how to do that.

"Lots of money," Benton said. "I'm brokering a deal with Fernando Montoya for a sweet piece of ass that could make all of us rich."

"Is that right?" I asked in a deceptively calm voice.

"Richard," the woman snapped. "Shut. Up."

"Sweet little girl," Richard said. "Hell, you help me get my hands on her, and all your boys can have a turn before we give her to Montoya. He won't care. I bet he'd love it if she were broken in for him."

Bull snarled and reached for the gun at his hip, but I caught his eye and shook my head.

"All of us, huh?" I asked.

Richard nodded. "She's a virgin too. Real fucking tight."

He had no idea just how much trouble he was in, and getting deeper with every word he uttered. Did the man not recognize Bull? Hell, we were all wearing our cuts that proudly displayed the Dixie Reapers logo. He really was a dumb shit.

"You can have her for as long as you like, fuck her over and over," Richard said. "Use her as much as you want, as long as you don't leave scars. Montoya has a thing about scars on his girls. She's real young too. Bet you guys like that shit, don't you?"

I moved closer, bracing my hands on the arms of the chair he was tied to, got right in his fucking face. He smirked, thinking he'd struck a bargain. Fucker didn't have a damn clue.

"That tight little virgin you want my entire club to fuck like some whore happens to be my old lady. And she sure as fuck isn't a virgin anymore. Might be carrying my baby even now, as often as I've filled her with my cum."

His face paled and his eyes went wide.

"Now here's how this is going to go down. I've seen the videos, know you've been watching my girl since she was just a damn kid. And I've seen Montoya's site with some of those same videos, offering her to the highest bidder. Don't worry. He'll be taken care of. There's a special place in hell for sick fucks like him. But you... you and your whore of a wife aren't walking out of here. I protect what's mine, and Ridley is fucking mine."

Marsha Benton whimpered, and I switched my attention to her.

"Oh, don't worry, Mrs. Benton. I may have plans for you, but they aren't anywhere near what you deserve. What I should do is sell you to some shithole whorehouse, make sure you're fucked morning, noon, and night, until you contract some flesh-eating disease that makes you die slowly and painfully. Would you like that? To be made into a whore just like you were going to do to your nineteen-year-old daughter?"

"Please," she begged. "I'll do anything."

My lip curled in disgust.

"You can... you can fuck me," she offered. "Anywhere and anyhow you want. Just let me go."

The laugh that rumbled out of me was hard and cold. "My baby girl is waiting in bed for me right now. Already fucked her before coming here to deal with this shit, and you think I'd ever want to touch you? The fucking bitch who sold her? You're her mother. You were supposed to love and protect her. But you never did, did you? You just made sure Bull didn't get custody because you wanted to make his life miserable. Or were you always planning on using Ridley in some way?"

Tears streaked her cheeks and she began to openly sob. Richard was quiet and deathly pale, staring at the floor. It seemed he'd already accepted that he wasn't going to live much longer. As much as I wanted to put both of these fuckers in the ground, I could tell that Bull wanted his pound of flesh for what had been done to his daughter. Wire hadn't let him see the videos, but Bull had been told what was on them. The man had nearly torn the clubhouse to shreds in his fury.

"Why don't you two teach Mrs. Benton the error of her ways?" I asked. "I think I'd like a little alone time with Mr. Benton."

Marsha began blubbering to Bull, begging him to spare her life. Bitch didn't seem to understand that the moment she'd betrayed her daughter, she'd signed her death sentence. Tank grabbed his special tools while Bull began dragging her into a dark corner. I didn't need to see what would happen to know she'd be punished adequately, and would never draw another fucking breath.

"Tell me something, Benton," I said as I perused the tools left on the dirty table nearby. "Did you get off on watching Ridley all those years? Sick bastard that you are, I bet you jerked off countless times to those videos, even when she was nothing more than a kid."

He remained quiet, but I could see the truth in his eyes when he looked at me. Yeah, the sick fuck had gotten off on watching her. It was almost a pity he had to die. Death seemed too nice for someone like him. I wanted him to suffer endlessly for his crimes, but I wasn't about to let him roam free. Not only would my woman be in danger, but others probably would be too. His sick obsession made me wonder something.

"She's not your first, is she? Oh, you may have only watched Ridley, but you did more with the others. I'm sure of it. You didn't just stumble across Montoya and offer him a deal. How many? How many young girls have you bought from him?"

The man didn't answer, but he didn't have to. Yeah, I was about to do the world a fucking favor by taking this asshole out. He was nothing but a rapist who preyed on young girls. Didn't matter if he paid for the services through some fucked-up website. He was a sick fuck and needed to be put down.

"Here's what I'm going to do. I'm going to have a little fun with you, and if you can keep from screaming, I'll end your life quicker. But I'm really hoping you're going to scream."

I pulled off my cut and my shirt. He watched my movements, but kept silent.

"Don't want your blood all over my cut and favorite shirt. Bad enough I'll probably have to throw out these jeans when I'm done," I told him.

Marsha's screams echoed around us, but the sick fuck in front of me didn't seem bothered that his wife was being tortured. I had no doubt he'd have offered her on a silver platter if he thought it would get him out of this, no matter what we did to her. She might have offered sexual favors, but no one volunteered for the pain she was feeling right now. No matter what thoughts were going through Richard's mind, there was no walking away from what he'd done.

He visibly swallowed, and the wet stain on the front of his pants grew. Sissy-ass fucker had pissed himself again. I picked up a pair of grips and stopped in front of him. My gaze didn't leave his face as I reached for one of the hands tied down to the chair. Gripping the end of his nail, I ripped it out of the nail bed and watched as he fought to control himself. Blood dripped from his finger onto the floor, and I didn't give him even a second to breathe before I ripped out another one.

I had to give it to the fucker, he was holding strong, but I'd only just begun. I took my time and finished removing his nails before starting on his teeth. He whimpered and tears streaked his face, but he still wouldn't scream. Bull and Tank stepped back into the light, both covered in blood.

"Bitch is fucking dead," Bull said.

"We made sure she didn't go easy," Tank said. "Any mother who would sell their kid into prostitution deserves what she got and then some."

Bull came over and placed a hand on my shoulder. "I know you want to watch the light die out in his eyes, that you want to be the one to put him in the ground, but don't take that shit back to my daughter. Why don't you let me and Tank handle this? I promise he won't go for a long time yet. We'll draw it out as long as possible, make sure he suffers. But you have Ridley waiting for you."

I looked from Bull to Tank and then nodded. As much as I wanted to be the one to end the sorry fucker's life, they were right. My woman was waiting for me, and there would be enough shit to deal with in our lives without me killing her mom and stepdad. I wiped the blood off my hands before grabbing my shirt and cut.

"Stop by the clubhouse and shower and change," Tank said. "Ridley might freak out when she sees you."

I looked down at the blood splattered on my jeans and encrusted around my nails. "Yeah, I'll do that."

"Venom, my little girl doesn't need to know what happened to her momma and stepdad. You just make sure she knows they aren't coming after her anymore. Leave the details out of it," Bull said. "She's not used to this way of life."

"I'd never do anything to hurt her," I said. "It's inevitable that club shit will touch her life in some way, but what happened here today stays between the three of us and the Pres. No one else needs to know."

Bull nodded and turned back toward Benton. I strode outside and climbed onto my bike. When I reached the clubhouse, no one asked questions and gave me a wide berth as I went back to my room. I showered and pulled on clean clothes before I went home to my woman. When I pulled into the driveway, I turned off the bike and stared at the house a moment. It was quiet, the taint of what was happening across the compound not having touched it. And it sure as fuck wouldn't touch Ridley either.

I let myself into the house and followed my nose to the kitchen, where a fresh pot of coffee was on the counter. Ridley was dressed and sitting at the kitchen table, a steaming cup of coffee in her hands. I poured myself a cup and sat on a chair next to my woman. She didn't ask where I'd been or what I'd been doing. Just gave me a smile and took a sip from her cup. Even though I got her plenty dirty in the bedroom, she still looked like my angel, the sun glinting off her golden hair. Her eyes still held an innocence that I hoped she never lost. I might fuck her every way imaginable, and she might be the property of a dirty old biker, but there was a goodness to Ridley that I thought would always shine brightly.

"Did you do what I said?" I asked.

Her cheeks flushed and she nodded. "Sitting is… interesting. But I didn't know how long you'd be gone so I didn't want to just lie in bed all day."

My gaze trailed down her slender throat and lingered on her breasts. The way her nipples were poking through her shirt, I wondered if she'd bothered to put on a bra. Maybe I'd make that a rule. Don't wear a bra in the house. I liked the idea of being able to pull up her shirt and have instant access to those pink nipples. Sitting in that chair, she was at the perfect height for me to push them together and slide my dick between the plump mounds, fuck those gorgeous tits until I came all over her.

My cock hardened in my jeans just thinking about it.

"That look on your face," she murmured. "Whatever you just thought about, you should do it."

"What look?" I asked, my gaze still fastened on her chest.

"The hungry look that says you want to do something naughty to me, but for some reason you're holding back."

"You wearing a bra, baby girl?"

"No," she said softly.

I pushed back my chair and came to stand next to her, turning her to face me. Without a word, I pulled her shirt over her head, watching her breasts bounce when they were freed. Ridley spread her legs, and I moved in closer, reaching for my belt buckle. I unfastened my pants and opened them enough to pull out my cock. This wasn't going to work unless my dick was wet first. I touched her bottom lip and got her to drop her jaw. Feeding her my cock an inch at a time, I didn't stop until I was balls deep. I thrust a few times, getting my shaft nice and slick, before I pulled free.

I adjusted my stance and pressed her breasts together before sliding my dick between them. Ridley's eyes went wide a moment, and then she looked down to watch. With every upward thrust, my dick kissed her lips.

"Open, baby. Show me how much you love this cock."

Ridley opened her mouth, her tongue flicking out to tease me with every stroke. I pumped hard and fast, mesmerized by the sight. My dick looked good fucking her like this, and it made me fucking hot when her mouth closed over me with every thrust. When I was close to coming, I decided I wanted to see my cum on her lips and plunged deep until I started coming. Most of it spurted into her mouth, but I pulled out and painted her lips with the rest. She swallowed it all and licked her lips clean.

"Take off those jeans, baby girl, and get your ass up on this table."

She stood and shimmied out of her tight ass jeans, then sat on the edge of the table. I didn't bother zipping up before I sat in the chair she'd just vacated. Her legs were sprawled on either side of me, that pretty pussy of hers open and so damn wet. I could see where my cum had dried on her earlier and fuck if I didn't want to add more to it. I pushed her thighs wider apart and patted her slick little lips with my fingers.

"Who does this belong to?" I asked her.

"You. Only you."

I trailed my fingers through her slick folds before plunging them inside her. "Is all this cream for me? You been thinking about me, baby girl?"

"Yes," she said, biting back a moan.

"Were you thinking about the fucking I gave you this morning?"

Her cheeks turned pink and she shook her head.

"Was my naughty girl thinking about my cock in her ass?"

Her face flushed an even brighter red, and she nodded.

"That plug in your ass isn't quite so uncomfortable anymore, is it? Maybe I need to make another trip to that store. Get one that vibrates."

She whimpered, and fuck if she didn't get even wetter.

"I think my angel's a naughty girl who likes getting dirty."

"Please, don't make me wait, Venom."

"That ass of yours is still going to be tight. I'm not fucking it until I have the lube handy. Doesn't mean I can't make my baby feel good, though. Why don't you reach down here and spread that pussy wide for me?"

Her hand slipped between her legs and she spread her lips like I'd asked. She was so fucking pretty I could just stare at her for hours, all open and wet like this. I placed my mouth against her core, my tongue driving into her. Ridley cried out, and I felt her body tense. My hands pushed her thighs as wide as they would go as I feasted on her tender flesh. My tongue fucked her, lapping up all her cream, and making her beg for more. I knew what she wanted, but she was going to have to beg me for it.

I teased her, drawing out her pleasure. Every time I felt she was close to coming, I slowed down. My face was soaked, and her scent was driving me wild. She was laid out before me like a buffet, and I could have spent hours between her legs.

"Please, Venom," she begged.

I growled and ravaged her sweet pussy.

"Make me come," she pleaded.

My tongue delved deep and hard, again and again, and when I thought she couldn't take another moment of it, I sucked her clit into my mouth so hard she came with a keening cry. Ridley lay panting when I drew away and wiped off my face. I stood, readjusted my pants, then kicked the chair over in my haste. I scooped her into my arms and took the stairs two at a time. After I carried her to the bedroom and eased her down onto the mattress, I reached for my clothes to strip them off.

"Don't," she said softly.

My hands froze on the waist of my jeans, my dick poking through my open zipper. "Don't what, baby girl?"

"I liked you fucking me with your clothes on. It felt... I don't know."

"Felt dirty?" I asked.

She nodded.

"Hands and knees at the edge of the bed, baby girl. I'm going to give us what we both want."

She got into position and I pushed my pants down far enough my dick and balls were out. If she wanted me to fuck her with my clothes on, that's what I would do. Didn't matter to me if I was naked as long as I got to fuck my beautiful girl. I slowly removed the plug from her ass and set it aside, then squeezed a generous amount of lube onto her little hole, before slicking my cock.

I stroked her with my fingers, making sure she was nice and wet and oh-so-ready for me. Ridley pressed her head to the mattress and moaned, shoving her ass back at me. When I felt she was as prepared as she was going to get, I placed the head of my cock at her opening.

"Breathe, baby girl, and push out."

It took some work, but the head of my cock popped through the ring of muscle, and I took my time working my dick inside her. I palmed her ass cheeks, spreading them wide so I could watch as she stretched around my shaft.

"Fuck, baby. I think this is my new favorite thing. Am I hurting you?"

"No. I'm so full, but it doesn't hurt."

A few more thrusts and I was balls deep inside her. Christ, but it felt good. My cock jerked inside her, and I knew I wouldn't last too long. If I'd thought her pussy was tight, this was even better.

"You better hold on, baby girl. I'm about to ride this ass hard and deep. You tell me if I need to stop."

She made a soft sound I took as consent, and I began driving into her. I'd never felt anything so fucking incredible in my life. The sight of my cock fucking her was almost enough to make me come, but I'd be damned if I did before she'd gotten hers.

"Play with your clit, baby girl. Make yourself come. You're going to squeeze my cock so fucking good, aren't you?"

It didn't take her long before she was coming so hard I nearly saw stars with how tight she gripped me. I took her like a man possessed, driving into her again and again, until I'd fucked every bit of my cum into her ass. When I pulled out, I was breathing like I'd run a damn marathon, but my dick was still hard. My cum was so deep in her ass, I'd be willing to bet it would still be there tomorrow.

Ridley collapsed onto the bed and rolled onto her back.

"I didn't hurt you?" I asked.

"No. It felt... different, but a good different."

I braced myself over her and brushed my lips against hers. "I hope you don't have plans to leave this bed anytime soon."

"I'm sure you could persuade me to stay in bed."

"Oh yeah?" I smiled down at her.

"What if I told you I needed you again?"

I pushed away from the bed and stood up. Ridley spread her legs in invitation, and fuck if I was going to ignore it. I quickly stripped out of my clothes and cleaned myself up, then I spent the next several hours fucking the gorgeous woman I'd claimed for my own.

Chapter Nine

Ridley

It had been over a month since I'd come to the compound seeking refuge. I'd found so much more. Way more, I thought as I looked at the little stick on the bathroom counter. In all the weeks we'd been together, not once had Venom talked to me about kids. I'd known that if he kept taking me without protection that sooner or later I'd end up pregnant. I just wasn't certain if that had been his plan all along, or if he'd thought I was on the pill. Plenty of women took them, even if they weren't sexually active, but the hormones in them messed with my body, and my doctor had advised against them. I should have said something sooner, should have told him, but every time Venom touched me I couldn't think, only feel.

What the fuck was I going to do?

I buried the stick at the back of the bathroom drawer and hid the box in the bottom of the trash can. I would tell him, but I wasn't sure this was the right time. He'd been distant lately, as if something heavy weighed on his mind. It was probably just shit with the club, but I had to wonder.

Wire had turned over everything to the Feds like he'd said he would. My stepdad's crimes had been all over the news. Everyone now knew that Richard Benton III had been a sick man who preyed on young girls, had lost his family fortune, and had tried to sell his own stepdaughter as a way of fixing the situation. My name was kept out of the latest news and the search for me had ended, and for that I was thankful. But I knew the story that Mom and my stepdad had fled the country was false, and I wondered how many people would be willing to believe it. No one mentioned my stepmonster little brother, and while he was just a kid caught in a bad situation, I wasn't about to ask Venom to bring him here. Someone would take him in -- one of his relatives on the Benton side.

I'd seen the look on Venom's face when he'd watched those videos. No, my mom and stepdad hadn't fled like the news said. I might not know what really happened, but I had a feeling that if anyone went looking for Mom and Richard, they'd have to look six feet deep. Venom never mentioned it to me, and I never asked. As long as they were out of my life, I didn't much care. The woman had been my mother, and I should have felt something, but we'd never been close, and betrayal had killed any feelings I might have once had for her. I hoped she was roasting in hell.

The news didn't say anything about Fernando Montoya, though, and that worried me. The man had left me alone so far, and might not even know where I was hiding, but how long would that last? It frightened me, knowing that I now carried a life inside me, and that monster was still free. I knew Venom didn't want to get involved directly, was worried about the repercussions of going after a man like Montoya, but I didn't want to live in fear. I wanted to know that I was safe, that my baby was safe.

The door slammed downstairs, and I heard Venom's booted steps coming up the stairs. I met him in the bedroom, trying to keep the worry from my face. He looked haggard but determined. His lips brushed across mine, and he pulled me into his arms, just holding me. There was no place I loved more than being pressed against Venom with his arms around me. I always felt safe, protected, and even loved. He'd never said the L word to me, and maybe he never would. But it was there in his eyes when he looked at me, and that was enough.

"Rough day?" I asked.

"Something like that. Just got some bad news."

I pulled back and cupped his jaw. "Does it have to do with me?"

"You're safe, Ridley. I'm not going to let anyone get to you."

"It's Montoya, isn't it? He's still free."

Venom sighed and sank onto the edge of the bed. "I didn't want to bring this shit home to you."

"If I'm in danger, I need to know."

"The Feds aren't going after Montoya. Apparently, he's a small fish in an even bigger pond, and they're going for the top guy. No one even knew someone was pulling Montoya's strings, and fuck if I know what to do about it all."

"It's been a month," I reasoned. "Maybe he's forgotten about me."

His eyes were tortured as he looked at me.

"Or maybe not," I muttered.

"Wire has been keeping tabs on that site. The Feds and the Columbians managed to get it pulled down, but Montoya started another one. You're on there, Ridley, and it's so much fucking worse. With Richard and your mom gone, he knows the heat coming down on him has to do with you. He uploaded all the videos. Every fucking one. And the sick things he's posted... " Venom closed his eyes. "Fuck!"

"What does this mean for me? For us?" I asked softly.

"The things he's offering those men, what he said they could do to you... the bidding is in the millions, baby girl. That man isn't going to sit back and let you slip through his fingers."

My heart hammered in my chest. "You have to go after him, Venom. I know you're worried about the club and the heat it could bring down on your guys, but you have to stop him. Permanently."

"Ridley..."

I hadn't planned to tell him like this, but I grabbed his hand and placed it over my belly.

He stared a moment, his brow furrowed, then he gazed up at me in wonder. "You're pregnant?"

"Yeah. So it's not just my life on the line anymore, Venom. If he finds me, he'll probably kill your son or daughter. I love you, so damn much it hurts, and I never want anything bad to happen to you. But I need you to fight for our family."

Venom pulled me down onto his lap and kissed me fiercely. "I fucking love you, Ridley. You're mine, this baby is mine, and no one is ever going to hurt either one of you."

"So what are we going to do?" I asked.

"There has to be a way to take out Montoya without the club physically getting involved. I want this shit to stay away from our doorstep. It's no good for me to take the bastard out if it's only going to bring more danger within reach of you."

"Wire?" I asked.

He nodded. "Let's go see Wire."

When we reached the clubhouse, the place was packed. Music blasted and I could smell the sex and alcohol from outside. Seemed it was a rowdy night and I was about to see way more of the guys and the club sluts than I wanted. Venom gripped my hand and I focused on the back of his cut as we made our way back to Wire's room. Thankfully, I only saw a bare ass or two out of the corner of my eye before I was safely behind a closed door in Wire's sanctuary.

"You told her?" Wire asked. "What happened to keeping her in the dark while we figured this shit out?"

"She's pregnant," Venom said. "This shit needs to end now."

Wire ran a hand down his face. "All right. Look, I can fuck with the man's bank accounts, I can hack into his systems and wipe out the website, but those are just temporary things. The site will go back up, and he'll eventually figure out someone tampered with his accounts. They'll never find my trail, but there's no guarantee he won't tie the incidents to Ridley. It will just piss him off more."

"So there's nothing you can do?" I asked. "I just sit and wait for him to come for me?"

"No, baby girl." Venom squeezed my hand. "How much money do we have right now?"

Wire shrugged. "Roughly, a little over a million."

My eyes went wide. "You guys have over a million dollars?"

"Guns and drugs pay well," Wire said. "And that's just in the club account. Each member who helps with a job gets a cut."

Venom growled. "She doesn't need to know all that."

"Venom, I never thought you were an angel. I know what the one-percent patch on your cut means. You guys are outlaws, and I'm fine with that. As long as you come home to me every night in one piece, and your jobs don't endanger me and the baby, I don't care how you make your money." I frowned. "But you better not be selling those drugs to kids."

"We don't sell to them, but I can't guarantee the drugs don't end up in their hands anyway. I know you don't like it, baby girl, but it's just the way things are.

At least we aren't like Montoya and selling little girls. That shit's fucked up." Venom kissed my cheek. "Try not to worry about club business. I'll keep you safe, and that's all you need to worry about."

There wasn't much I could say to that. I'd agreed to this way of life when I'd told him to claim me, and I didn't regret it. I might not like how the club made its money, but he was right. There were worse ways of making a dollar.

"Why did you want to know how much we had?" Wire asked.

"Doesn't matter. It's not enough."

"For what?" I asked.

"I thought maybe we could put a hit on Montoya," Venom said. "The man needs to die, even if I don't get to pull the trigger myself."

"But you said there's someone bigger than him. What if that person comes after me?" I asked.

"They won't," Venom said. "I can't imagine Montoya's boss gives a shit about one woman who got away. This seems personal for Montoya. You made a fool of him by running away, and now he wants payback."

"We don't have money for a hit, but... " Wire's eyes narrowed. "We need Torch in here. There's another way to take care of Montoya, but the club will have to do something for it, something big."

"Wait here, baby girl," Venom said. He released my hand and left me alone with Wire. When he came back, the President was on his heels, his pants unfastened.

My cheeks flushed, and I averted my gaze.

"This better be fucking important," Torch said. "What couldn't wait?"

"I know how to take out Montoya for good," Wire said. "But the person who can handle the job is going to want something in return."

"What's he want?" Torch asked.

"Protection for his daughter."

"So have him bring her here. The boys can watch over her for a bit."

Wire shook his head. "Permanent protection."

"What the fuck does that even mean?"

"It means that my contact has offered to help us any time we want, no job too hard or too bloody, with one condition. He wants a property patch for his daughter."

"That fucker expects one of my guys to claim his daughter as an old lady?" Torch asked with a laugh. "He's got some fucking balls."

"Isabella is seventeen and away at boarding school. He's already made arrangements for her to stay until graduation," Wire said.

"She's just a kid," Torch shouted. "What the fuck, Wire? You expect one of the guys to claim a fucking kid?"

"No," Wire said. "I expect you to."

Torch became so still I wasn't certain he was breathing.

"Her father has arranged for her to visit family out of the country for a little while after she graduates, but when she returns to US soil, he wants her tied to you in every way possible. This isn't an in-name-only type deal. Shall we say he's familiar with your background and the work you've done for the MC over the years, and feels you're the best man to protect his only child."

"My background?" Torch asked, his gaze sharpening.

"He knows about your work prior to this way of life," Wire said. "Either you claim his daughter as your old lady, or he won't help us. Not now, and not ever. And we could really fucking use him."

"What's so special about this guy and his daughter?" I asked. She was only two years younger than me, and I was Venom's old lady and carrying his baby. It didn't seem so farfetched to me. They might call her a kid, but in some places she was already considered an adult.

"Ever hear of Casper VanHorne?" Wire asked, his gaze on Torch.

"Fucking hell," the President muttered. "Jesus. If Casper Fucking VanHorne is willing to do our dirty work, how the hell can I say no? The man's the goddamn Picasso of wet work. If anyone finds out he's on our side, no one will dare give us shit."

I'd seen enough movies to get an idea of what wet work meant, and apparently the man was a total badass. It sounded like agreeing to his terms would be good for the club. Still, Torch looked torn.

"His daughter's been taken a few times. Casper leaves her well-guarded, but it isn't always enough. Men can be bought for the right price. He knows no one is getting into this compound undetected, and if they did and Isabella was yours... " Wire shrugged. "Right now she has one badass who cares what happens to her. But as your old lady, she'd have you and every Dixie Reaper watching over her."

"Do you have a picture of Isabella?" I asked.

Wire grinned and pulled out his phone. He scrolled through some images and pulled up a picture of a girl so damn beautiful my eyes nearly hurt just looking at her. Torch stared at the image, perhaps a little too long. With his pants still open, he couldn't hide the erection he was sporting.

"Tell him he has a deal," Torch said. "Fucking hell. Like I ever wanted an old lady."

"Something tells me you might not mind that one so much," Venom said with a smile.

Torch shook his head and stormed out of the room, the door slamming behind him. Venom chuckled, and even Wire looked amused. Something told me there was more to the story than what I knew. But if Isabella's dad was going to take care of my problem, then I was more than happy for her to join the MC. I'd welcome her with open arms.

"She's a good kid," Wire said. "Quiet. A little shy. But I think she'll be a calming influence on Torch. Casper's been after me for months to set the deal up, but I didn't have a bargaining chip before now. Yeah, it would have been awesome to have him on our side, but something told me your girl being in trouble would be the push Torch needed."

"So it's over?" I asked.

Wire nodded. "It's as good as done. I'll place the call as soon as you leave, and Montoya will be out of the picture by tomorrow night."

"Come on, baby girl. Time to head home," Venom said.

Impulsively, I hugged Wire, which made Venom growl. My sexy biker pulled me closer, glared at his brother, then dragged me out of the clubhouse. I saw Torch in the corner of the room, throwing back shots. Poor man. He probably thought his life was over, having to claim Isabella, but I had a feeling that things were just beginning for him.

When we stepped out onto the porch, Venom pushed me against the side of the building and kissed me long and deep. I clutched at his cut as his mouth ravaged mine. Heat began curling through my body, and my pussy ached to be filled. Coming to the Dixie Reapers had been the best decision I'd ever made. I'd come to find my dad, and safety from the outside world, but had gotten everything I'd ever wanted.

"I love you, Venom," I whispered against his lips.

"Love you too, baby girl. And I'm going to show you how much all night long."

I smiled up at him and let him lead me over to his bike. If Venom promised to keep me up all night, I knew he meant it. The man was insatiable, and I fucking loved it. I hoped the passion we felt for one another would never die.

My hand splayed over my still flat belly. Even though it was way too soon to tell, I had a feeling we were having a daughter. I didn't know what she'd look like, but I knew I would love her with all my heart. It was my fondest wish that our child would one day find the love I'd found with Venom. Nothing beat being owned by a sexy as fuck biker with a possessive gleam in his eyes.

And if we had a boy... well, if he was anything like his daddy, there would be broken hearts all over.

Epilogue

Ridley

It had been two weeks since the news of Montoya's death had been splattered all over the papers and on the TV. I breathed a sigh of relief when I'd watched as the reporter talked about the child pornography found at his home, along with women who had been held captive and forced into prostitution. My nightmare was finally over. Well, the life-threatening one anyway.

Nausea had me clamping my hand over my mouth in an effort not to puke. Whoever called this shit morning sickness was an evil bastard, because as far as I could tell it was all-day sickness. The clubhouse was packed, and I refused to bolt to the bathroom unless it became dire. Casper VanHorne had arrived a short while ago with his stunningly beautiful daughter in tow.

When they'd arrived, Isabella had kept her gaze trained on the floor and meekly followed her father. I saw the contempt on some of the bikers' faces. They thought she was weak and pathetic, even if she was gorgeous. I heard whispers that she would ruin Torch. I didn't think they were right, though. Her back was straight, her shoulders back. There was pride in her stance, despite her lowered head. I didn't think she was weak at all, but Wire was right. The girl was shy.

While Casper spoke to Torch, I decided as the VP's old lady, it was my job to make Isabella feel welcome. Venom was somewhere nearby, probably watching me like a hawk. I strode across the room and stopped beside Isabella.

"I'm Ridley," I said, holding out my hand.

She looked up, surprise flashing in her eyes. "Isabella," she said, shaking my hand briefly.

"You're going to be Torch's old lady?" I asked.

She nodded, casting a quick glance at the biker in question. Her cheeks flushed.

Interesting.

I'd never given Torch much thought, but he was a nice-looking man. He was older, in his late-forties maybe, possibly a little older, but his black hair was still dark as pitch, and his gray eyes were attractive. When Isabella looked back at me, I saw what I'd been looking for. She might be young, and this might not have been a situation of her choosing, but she wanted Torch. There was a fire in her eyes that would serve her well when she finally joined us.

"I'm Venom's old lady," I told her. "The VP. I know you aren't staying right now, but when you come back, you'll have a friend here already."

A slight smile curled the corners of her lips. "I'd like that."

I leaned in a little closer. "Give him hell," I whispered.

Her smile broadened, and her face lit up. Yeah, this girl was going to go after what she wanted, and now that she'd seen Torch, the poor man was screwed. He had no idea how much his life had just changed.

Casper pulled Isabella forward to introduce her to Torch.

The second the President's eyes settled on her, I knew he was as done for as Venom. My sexy biker stepped up behind me, curling an arm around my waist.

"Are you causing trouble?" he whispered in my ear.

"Maybe just a little. But it's going to be so much fun to watch the sparks fly between those two."

He chuckled and rubbed his beard against my neck. "I think you might be right. Come on, baby girl. I don't think we're needed for now."

I couldn't stop the smile that spread across my face. I didn't know how long it would be until Isabella returned to us, but I was looking forward to it. The big, bad president of one of the fiercest MCs in the country was about to be taken down by a girl half his size. But once the dust settled, I didn't think he'd mind it too much.

"Take me home, Venom."

"Oh, I plan on it. I hope you slept well."

"And why is that?"

He growled and swung me up into his arms. "Because I'm going to spend the rest of the day and night driving my cock into your sweet pussy until you scream my name. And when you're too sore to take me again, I'm going to flip you over and fuck your tight little ass again and again."

"You know I love it when you talk dirty to me."

"Oh, baby girl, you have no idea just how dirty I can be."

Torch (Dixie Reapers MC 2)

Harley Wylde

Isabella: I was seventeen when my daddy gave me to Torch, who inked me, kissed me, then watched me walk away. I was supposed to return after I graduated, but instead I ran. Now I'm back, ready to face whatever fate awaits me. He's probably pissed, and rightly so. It was only supposed to be a short separation, but three years have passed. I expected yelling, maybe some public humiliation. It never occurred to me he'd kiss me so deeply, so passionately that I'd be begging for more. He'll be my first, my last, my only... because I'm his, and he's never going to let me forget it.

Torch: For years, I've kept my distance, watching over the girl I claimed as my own. She wears my brand, and I know it's only a matter of time before she comes home. I remembered a stunning young woman, but it's a siren who walks back through my door, all luscious and curvy. There may be about thirty years between us, but fuck if I care what people think. I want her. She's mine, and I'm going to remind her of that. I'll take her any way I can, as often as I can, and when I'm done, she'll never again think of walking out the door. Because what she doesn't know is she's done the impossible... she's claimed the heart of a man who didn't think he had one. Now that she's worked her way deep inside, I'll rain down hell on anyone who tries to keep us apart. No one's going to come between us, especially not the man who gave his daughter to me -- not even if he has the entire cartel army on his ass.

Prologue

Torch
Three Years Ago

This was absolutely fucking insane. I couldn't believe I'd agreed to brand some girl as my old lady. Fuck, she wasn't even legal yet. What the hell was I supposed to do with some seventeen-year-old girl who was still in high school? At forty-eight, I was old enough to be her dad. Shit, I was probably older than her dad. But Casper VanHorne had come through for my club, so I would abide by the agreement.

When he entered the clubhouse, it was like the room dropped twenty degrees. The man was cold and calculating, an absolute bastard who had no problem taking someone out by any means necessary. And from what I'd heard, he was damn good at his job. Word on the street was Casper was the country's top-paid assassin. His gun was for hire, no job too big or too small, as long as the price was right. And the price he'd asked was that I protect his daughter and make her my old lady.

"Torch," Casper said, reaching out to shake my hand. "I'm glad you agreed to my terms."

"You didn't give me much choice. It was either risk my VP's old lady, or agree, and since Ridley is carrying Venom's child, it wasn't a choice at all."

Casper smiled, the sight chilling me. He reached back and pulled a young girl forward, her head tipped down as she gazed at the floor. She was slender and pale, her ebony hair hanging in curls around her face and down her back. Reminded me a little of Snow White.

"Isabella, mind your manners. Say hello to your husband-to-be."

Fuck if that thought didn't make me ill.

Her face lifted, and I forgot to fucking breathe for a moment. Her blue eyes were the color of the sky on a cloudless day, but what held me spellbound, was the intensity of her gaze. She might be a kid, but this was a kid who had seen far too much. A slight smile curled the corners of her lips. I'd thought she was beautiful in her picture, but in real life she was so much more.

"Hello," she said. Her voice was light and reminded me of fairies and shit.

"Hello, Isabella."

"Is everything ready?" Casper asked.

I nodded and motioned for them to follow me to the back. Zipper had already set up his work station, and I'd given him a basic design. Now that I'd met the girl, I knew she deserved something better. While she sat in the chair and her father roamed the room, I pulled Zipper into the hall.

"What is it, Pres?"

"That design. It's not going to work."

Zipper smiled. "Need something a little more feminine? She's a dainty little thing, isn't she?"

Yeah, she was fucking dainty all right. I only hoped when the time came to claim her I didn't break her. Christ, but I hoped her father didn't expect things to go that far today. The thought of bedding a child -- even one as gorgeous as Isabella -- made me ill, even if she was nearly eighteen.

"I can freehand something, make it up as I ink her. If you trust me," Zipper said.

"I've seen your work. Do what you think is best. I want something that complements her." Poor girl was just as much a pawn in this as I was, if not more so. No reason to make things unpleasant for her.

Zipper nodded, and we went back into his work room. Isabella looked a little pale, and I noticed her father was standing across the room from her. Was he seriously not even going to hold his little girl's hand? She looked fucking terrified as she looked at the tattoo equipment.

I pulled an empty chair over beside her and laced our fingers together. Her hand trembled in mine, but she gave me a tentative smile. When the needle first touched her arm, she cried out and tensed up.

"Easy, baby," I soothed. "Breathe."

She nodded, but I noticed the tears gathered in her eyes. I gave her hand a squeeze, and she seemed to settle a little. Her head turned toward the arm being tattooed, and I reached up and turned her face back toward me.

"Look at me, not at the tattoo."

"All right," she said softly.

There was something about this girl that made me want to protect her. She seemed fragile, delicate... there was an otherworldliness about her, like a fairy or angel had been dropped into my lap. As aggravated as I was over the situation, I knew it wasn't her fault, and I wasn't about to take my frustration out on her. She deserved better than that.

"You're being very brave," I told her.

She shook her head. "I'm not. I'm far from brave. If I were brave, I wouldn't need your protection."

Her words intrigued me. Casper had said his daughter needed protection, but I'd never thought to ask from what. Had something happened to her? I'd thought maybe Casper was just being an ass about the entire thing, but maybe I was wrong. If there was a reason she needed me, then I wanted to know what it was.

"Baby, why do you think you wouldn't need my protection if you were braver?"

"Because I..." She bit her lip and tears formed in her eyes again.

"Because what?"

"She's not tough enough," Casper said over my shoulder. "My enemies have tried to use her against me. Last time it was taken too damn far."

My gaze never left Isabella's, and I could see the pain in her eyes, and the shame. "What did they do to you, baby?"

"She doesn't need to relive that shit, Torch," Casper said, his voice a near growl.

"She's fucking mine now, right?" I glared at him over my shoulder. "So get the fuck out so I can talk to her."

Casper glanced at his daughter, then left the room. After the door shut, I turned back toward the beautiful girl with the haunted eyes. Whatever had happened to her, it hadn't been good. I didn't like that someone had hurt someone so pure. Just looking at her you could tell she was completely innocent. I'd never met anyone like her before, and part of me hoped that innocence would never be extinguished, even though I knew that wasn't realistic.

"What happened when you were taken?" I asked.

"They stripped my clothes off me and locked me in a cold room with just a concrete floor and a cot. They gave me a pot to..." Her cheeks flushed.

I didn't like where this was going, but I needed to know everything. "You're safe here. No one's going to hurt you. Are those men coming after you again?"

"Not them, but others. Those men, they... they touched me. They sent a video to my dad and told him what would happen to me if he didn't do as they said."

"And what did your dad do?" I asked.

The tears dried up. "He killed them all."

"Good."

She smiled a little.

"Ink's done," Zipper announced barely forty-five minutes later. His voice sounded tight with emotion, and I knew it had been painful for him to hear her story. He'd never been able to stomach violence against women and children.

The script on her arm was beautifully done in blues and purples. Zipper had added what looked like twinkling lights around the *Property of Torch -- Dixie Reapers MC President* words in pinks, yellows, and greens. It was delicate and nicely done.

Zipper told her how to care for the tattoo, then put some ointment on it and wrapped it for her. I stood and helped Isabella out of the chair, but her legs buckled when she tried to stand. My arm went around her as a reflex, and her small body pressed against mine. The fact my dick started getting hard shouldn't have surprised me, not after my reaction to seeing her picture before, but it made me sick to my stomach. What the fuck was wrong with me? Yeah, she felt like a woman, but she was just a kid still. Isabella stared up at me, all sweetness and innocence, and I knew I was going to hell for what I was about to do, but fuck if I didn't need to taste her just once.

My lips closed over hers, and I could tell immediately she'd never been kissed. I coaxed her through it, my mouth caressing hers slowly. I kept the kiss simple, but hell if it didn't rock me. Countless women had kissed me over the years, but none were as sweet as Isabella. I'd promised her dad I wouldn't take another woman to my bed once I made Isabella my old lady, but now that I'd tasted her, I knew no one would ever compare anyway. When I took my dick in my hand, it would be her eyes I saw, her lips I tasted.

Yeah, I was going to hell.

I pulled away, and she clung to me.

"I promise you, Isabella, no one will ever hurt you. You're mine, and I will fucking kill anyone who tries to take you away. I know you have graduation to go through, and your dad said you're visiting family after that, but you come home anytime you're ready."

She nodded and stepped into the hall where her dad waited.

Zipper sadly shook his head.

"What the fuck is that supposed to mean?" I asked.

"You want her," Zipper said. "I was going to feel sorry for you, trapped in a relationship with some young girl. But she's not what we thought she'd be, is she?"

"No." I looked down the hall, where her dad was leading her away. "She's not."

If I'd known how damn long it would be before she decided to come home, I would have never let her leave.

Chapter One

Isabella

The car that had delivered me to my destination took off down the road like the hounds of hell were after it. Not that I could blame the poor driver. I looked through the gates at the Dixie Reapers MC compound. Not much had changed since I was last here. A Prospect approached the gates, his face lighting up when he saw me. I got that reaction a lot. I'd always been pretty, but the last few years I'd gained some womanly curves and my face had matured. He swaggered closer, his hand tucked into his belt.

"You looking for a good time?" he asked. "Because I could fuck you all night long, sweet thing."

I fought the urge to roll my eyes. Yeah, I'd never heard that one before.

"Open the gates," I demanded, trying to sound tougher than I was.

He licked his lips, apparently thinking he was getting his fondest wish. The gate slid open, and I strolled through on my heeled boots that hugged my calves and stopped just below my knees. The gate closed behind me, and the Prospect placed his hand on my waist. I quickly removed it.

"Why don't you get on your knees and give my cock some attention?" he said, starting to unfasten his belt.

"Or you could keep your pants zipped and your dick attached," I said.

"Did you just threaten to remove my dick?"

"Oh, I won't be the one removing it. Torch will."

He sneered at me. "And why would Torch give a shit about some whore who showed up uninvited?"

I held up my forearm, the brand that said *Property of Torch* clearly on display. I'd been marked when I was seventeen. My dad hadn't wanted to take a chance Torch would back out of the deal later. Because I'd been underage and a virgin, Dad had refused to let Torch claim me in any other way, but I was his just the same. And I'd damn sure never told my dad about the kiss I'd shared with Torch. That kiss had remained with me all these years. I still could taste him when I closed my eyes.

The Prospect's face paled, and he stammered an apology before getting out of my way. I walked across the concrete lot and up the clubhouse steps. Music blared from inside, and I braced myself for what I might find on the other side of the door. I'd heard my daddy threaten Torch if he so much as unzipped his pants with another woman. Casper VanHorne hadn't been fucking around. As far as he was concerned, Torch was married to me, and my daddy expected him to be faithful, even if I had been too young at the time. My heart ached at the thought that he might not have kept his promise. The moment I'd laid eyes on Torch, I'd fallen under his spell, and it had scared the hell out of me. It had scared me so much, I'd done the chicken shit thing and run.

I'd been gone a lot longer than I'd expected. My graduation had taken place within six months of Torch branding me as his. The plan had been for me to visit family abroad for six months, then return to Torch. I'd have been eighteen by then, nearly nineteen, and it would have been legal for us to be together, but I'd been too damn scared to come back. I'd only met him the one time, but the way he'd made me feel still shook me to my core. So, I'd hidden. Not just from Torch, but from my dad too. I'd used what few contacts I had and disappeared, making sure I left no trace, until I was ready to face my fate. Not an easy feat with two powerful men looking for you. I'd gotten fake documents with a new name and changed locations every few months. Staying under the radar hadn't been easy, but I'd managed.

I was twenty now, almost twenty-one, and I knew I couldn't keep running. Wasn't even certain I wanted to. I was a grown woman now, and it was time to claim my man. Or more likely, let him claim me. Assuming he wasn't pissed beyond belief. My hand pressed against the door. My future, whether good or bad, lay on the other side. I wouldn't blame Torch for being furious with me for being gone so long, for just vanishing. I knew my father was enraged, but I'd deal with Daddy later. But Torch... I belonged to him. I didn't know what the punishment would be for my actions, and I only hoped I was strong enough to take it. I'd probably made him look like a fool by taking off like that. It hadn't been my intention, but I didn't know if he'd care why I'd left the way I did.

I blew out a breath and opened the door, stepping inside the dimly lit interior. Smoke filled the air and nearly made me choke. Through the haze I could see the bikers weren't too picky about where they had sex. Naked women strolled through the room, completely on display for anyone to look at or touch. I hoped I hadn't made a mistake in coming here. Daddy had made a deal, and it was up to me to keep it, but I wasn't too happy with what I saw.

Torch was in the back corner with some of his brothers, a naked whore on his lap. She didn't seem to be doing much but sitting there, but it still made me ill. He was supposed to be mine. Part of me wanted to march over there, drag her ass off him, and kick her out the door. But I'd never been the confrontational sort. Even after all this time, I was still on the quiet side most days. I made my way over to the bar and climbed onto one of the stools. If I was going to get through this night, I knew I'd need a stiff drink. I cursed myself as a coward, thinking I didn't do justice to the VanHorne name. According to my daddy, I took after my mom, and since she hadn't been able to handle Dad's lifestyle and had died by her own hand when I was just a baby, I didn't think that was a compliment.

"Rum and coke," I told the Prospect behind the bar. "Heavy on the rum."

He winked and set about making my drink, then slid it in front of me. I downed it in a few swallows and motioned for another. A hand slid around my body and cupped my breast, squeezing it to the point of pain. I inhaled sharply and immediately wished I hadn't. Whoever was standing behind me smelled ripe, even over the smoke in the air.

"Whores aren't allowed to wear clothes in here," a voice slurred in my ear. "Strip and show me a good time."

"Good thing I'm not a whore," I said, removing his hand.

"Fucking bitch," he spat. "You aren't allowed to say no. Club rules."

He jerked me off the stool and backhanded me across the face. My knees nearly gave out, but he still gripped my arm tight. I could feel him bruising my skin even as pain radiated across my cheek.

I saw stars for a moment, and when he reached his hand back again, I reached up and grabbed it before it could connect with my face. His gaze focused on my arm and his glassy eyes went wide. He looked from my tattoo over to where I'd last seen Torch, and the blood drained from his face. I heard the sound of several booted feet heading toward us and braced for whatever was about to happen.

"Boy," a voice growled behind me. "We don't hit women around here."

That voice. I closed my eyes a moment, a shiver raking down my spine. All these years and I hadn't forgotten his voice. Even now, that voice made me want to submit, to give him anything he asked for.

"I didn't mean it, Pres. I didn't know she was yours."

I felt a warm hand on my waist, and slowly I was turned to face Torch. His gaze studied my face, sliding down my body. I could tell I was familiar to him, but he hadn't yet figured out who I was. I'd changed, matured, over the last three years. The stick-thin waif who had shown up here didn't exist anymore. When he saw the *Property of Torch* tattoo on my forearm, his gaze jerked back up to mine. I'd expected to see irritation when he realized who I was, but his gaze softened and the tenderness in the depths of his gray eyes left me breathless.

"Isabella," he said in a near whisper. His touch was gentle as he stroked my cheek where the asshole had hit me. That simple gesture was enough to make me feel foolish for running for so long. The feeling of his fingers against my skin made me want to curl into his chest and hold on tight. From the moment I'd first met him, I'd known Torch would keep me safe.

"I didn't know, Torch," the man blubbered. "I'd have never touched her if I'd known."

Torch's gaze was steady on mine another moment. When he looked at the man behind me, a coldness filled his eyes that chilled me to the bone. His touch remained gentle on me as he pulled me against his body, but his hand shot over my shoulder, and I heard the crack of his fist against the man's face. Brothers began gathering around us, and I hid my face against Torch's chest. This wasn't how I wanted everyone to meet me again after all this time.

"Get this fucker out of here," Torch said.

"Want me to teach him a lesson?" a man asked.

"Yeah, Tank. Why don't you show him what happens when you lay your hands on a woman. Especially *my* fucking woman."

The room grew so damn quiet I could have heard a pin drop. I looked up into Torch's face, and he was fiercely scowling at anyone nearby. I felt the power rippling through him as I clutched at his waist, my hands gripping the sides of his cut. Being near him almost made it hard for me to breathe. I knew when he finally touched me, more than the slight stroke against my cheek, when he truly made me his, it would change me forever. And that scared the hell out of me.

Torch's gaze dropped to mine, and there was a flash of fury in his eyes. His hand cupped my injured cheek. "Get me some ice," he barked at the Prospect behind the bar.

When he was handed an ice pack, he laid it against my cheek. I couldn't help but wince.

"I'm sorry, baby," he said. "It's already swelling, and it may bruise. What did that fucker say to you before he hit you?"

"He told me whores didn't get clothes, said I wasn't allowed to say no, and when I told him I wasn't a whore, he pulled me off the stool and hit me," I told him softly.

Torch growled. "Tank," he called out to the man who was quickly heading out the door.

"Yeah, Pres," he said, coming back to stand next to us.

"Bust that fucker's balls. Make sure his dick doesn't work for a while."

Tank smiled grimly. "You got it. Welcome home, Isabella."

My gaze didn't stray from Torch's face. There were a few more lines around his eyes than had been there before, and his hair had turned more silver, along with his beard. But he was still as devastatingly handsome as he'd been before. Maybe even more so. As his arm slid around my waist, I felt like I was finally where I belonged.

I heard murmurs around the room, then some whore started whining. "Why's he touching her when he could have me?" the woman bitched.

I closed my eyes, but Torch lifted my chin and I opened them again.

"Don't listen to her," he said. "I kept my word to your dad. No one's been in my bed since I put my mark on you."

I smiled faintly. "Afraid he'd cut off your balls?"

Humor flashed in his eyes. "Something like that."

"I haven't been with anyone either. I'm sorry it took me so long to come home, but I wasn't ready. I know you were looking for me, Dad was too, but I had some growing up to do. I've spent my entire life being protected and sheltered, everything given to me, my every move dictated. Being on my own opened my eyes a little." I bit my lip. "And maybe I was a little afraid you'd consume me when I got here. I just needed some time."

"Are you ready now?" he asked.

I nodded.

"That's all I fucking needed to know," he said, then his lips were on mine. His tongue thrust into my mouth, and he pressed me tight against his body, his cock grinding against me. For a moment, I was taken back to the day we'd met. Torch had kissed me, nothing like this kiss, but it had been my first ever. My only. I'd been his from that moment on, and not just because of the ink on my arm. "You're mine, baby. I've waited for three fucking years to claim you, and I'll be damned if I'm waiting a minute longer. You even think of walking out the door and disappearing again, and I will tie your ass to the bed."

My cheeks warmed. "I'm not going anywhere."

Torch kept his gaze on me as he addressed the room. "I'm taking my girl home. Any of you fuckers disturb me for the next twenty-four hours, and I will kick your sorry asses."

Without another word, he swung me up into his arms and began striding through the clubhouse and out the front door. There was a line of bikes outside, and he approached the one on the end. Torch eased me down his body and pointed to the bike. My leg swung over the seat, and once he'd climbed on, I pressed myself close to his back, my thighs embracing his body as my arms went around his waist. His body was hard and solid. My hands drifted down his abdomen and I felt the hardness of his cock pressing against his zipper.

Torch growled and put my hand back on his stomach. "You touch me when I say you can."

His words sent a thrill through me, and I rested my cheek against his back. The bike roared to life and soon we were flying down the road. His house wasn't too far, and he pulled to a stop in front of a two-story home that looked like it had been freshly painted.

There were flowering shrubs lining the front porch. It was… cute. And not something I pictured the badass President of Dixie Reapers MC owning.

"It's blue," I said.

"Like your eyes," he said.

He'd painted his house to remind him of my eyes? Nothing could have stunned me more. I got off the bike, and he practically dragged me up the steps and to the front door. Torch unlocked it, pulled me inside, then slammed the door shut and twisted the bolt. I looked around, taking in the warm maple floors and neutral-colored walls. This was my home now, and oddly, I felt like I belonged here.

"Upstairs. Now."

I climbed the stairs, my legs trembling with every step. The door at the end of the hall stood open, and I moved toward it. It was a spacious bedroom done in black, gray, and white. The bed was larger than any I'd seen before, and my cheeks flushed because I knew he was about to claim me. I'd held onto my virginity, not letting anyone touch me because I knew I belonged to him.

Something hit the floor behind me, and I turned, my eyes going wide when I saw Torch removing his clothes. I took in every inch that was exposed, and a warmth spread through me. Anyone looking at him wouldn't know he was in his fifties. His biceps bulged, his broad chest led down to a tapered waist and a set of abs I longed to touch. When his pants dropped, and I saw his cock for the first time, I couldn't stifle my moan. It was so hard and thick, so damn long. I balked for a moment, worrying it wouldn't fit.

"Take off your clothes, Isabella."

The command in his tone had me removing my clothes, even though my hands shook. I'd never been naked in front of anyone on purpose before. Just the one time those men had taken me, and I'd been humiliated and terrified. But Torch didn't make me feel either of those things. Excitement buzzed under my skin because I was finally going to be with the man I'd thought of every day for the last three years. It had been cowardly of me to stay away, but I was here now, and I had no doubt I would be his in every way before the sun came up.

As the last of my clothes fell to the floor, Torch walked around me, studying every inch of my body. He stopped in front of me, and the desire in his eyes took my breath away. I almost begged him to touch me, but I held back. The man in front of me wasn't one to take orders.

"Sit on the edge of the bed and lie back," he said.

I nodded and moved over to the big bed. I sat on the edge, then lay back against the cool bedding.

Torch moved closer, his gaze caressing me from head to toe.

"Spread your legs," he demanded. "I want to see what's mine."

My heart hammered in my chest as I slowly parted my thighs. I felt the cool air touch my pussy and wondered if he liked the fact I'd had it waxed. I'd known what would happen when I came to him, and I'd wanted to be prepared. The girls I'd gone to school with had always giggled and talked about how their boyfriends liked them smooth.

Torch stared, his gaze hungry. His hands reached for me, his palms sliding up my thighs, then pushing my legs farther apart. I felt my pussy open to his heated gaze, and I flushed from head to toe. I'd never been so exposed before, but this was Torch and I was his.

"No one's touched you?" he asked.

"No."

His gaze met mine. "You ever make yourself come?"

I slowly shook my head. I'd tried a few times, but I hadn't been able to get there.

"Then I guess we'd better rectify that," he said, getting to his knees. His hands still held me wide-open, and as he leaned closer, I felt his hot breath blow across me. My thighs tensed a moment before his lips touched me.

Nothing could have prepared me for the feel of Torch's lips against my pussy. His tongue stroked the soft skin before plunging inside. I gasped as his tongue flicked in and out of my tight channel, my nipples hardening from the intense sensations rolling over me. His hands still held me wide-open as his mouth ravaged me. The soft hair of his beard just heightened the experience. His tongue speared me again before circling my clit. My body felt like it was on fire, and I knew it was only going to get more intense. He'd barely gotten started, and I felt like I might detonate at any moment. His tongue dipped into my core again, then he sucked my clit into his mouth and I came, screaming his name. I could feel my release dripping onto the bedding, and I trembled from head to toe.

Torch bit my inner thigh, then rose over me. His nose traced mine, and then he placed his lips near my ear. "Next time you scream, it had better be Connor I hear on your lips. Only club whores scream out Torch."

I blinked up at him. "Connor?"

A slight smile graced his lips. "Guess your daddy never told you. My name's Connor Maguire.

But outside this house, or in front of other people, I'm Torch."

"All right," I said softly. It made me wonder what else I didn't know about the man who was going to claim me body and soul.

Chapter Two

Torch

She was so fucking beautiful, and she was mine. I'd known where she was the last three years, having Wire keep tabs on her, as well as my military buddies, but I'd given her some space. I'd had no doubt she'd come home when she was ready, and I'd tried to be a patient man. Even lied to her father's face when he'd been searching for her. But now, with her spread out before me, I was barely hanging on. If she ever walked out the door again, I'd track her down and make good on my threat. Her ass would be tied to the bed, and she'd stay there until I'd filled her so full of cum she'd be too damn pregnant to run anywhere.

I trailed kisses up her silky thigh, across her soft stomach, until my lips closed around the tip of one of her perky breasts. Her fingers tunneled through my hair, and she thrust upward, shoving more of the silky mound into my mouth. I chuckled and gave it a good, hard suck. Isabella moaned beneath me, and her hands tightened in my hair. It had been so damn long since I'd been with a woman, I hoped like fuck I didn't embarrass myself the minute I got inside her. A man's hand just wasn't a good enough substitute for a hot, wet pussy.

I released her nipple and crawled farther up her body, closing my lips over hers. Her tongue tangled with mine, and I gave a soft growl as the head of my cock brushed against her slick folds. With a flex of my hips, I rubbed my cock up and down her wet lips, loving the fact she seemed to get more drenched by the minute. Every stroke bumped her clit and made her squirm just a little bit more. When I couldn't hold back another moment, I slowly started to sink into her.

Isabella's fingers tightened on me.

"Breathe, baby," I murmured. It was going to hurt, and there wasn't a damn thing I could do about it. I wasn't exactly small, and her virgin pussy was the tightest damn thing I'd ever felt.

She stared up at me, complete trust in her eyes, as I used small, short thrusts to work my length into her channel. When I pushed into her fully, tears slipped down her cheeks, but she didn't make a sound. I kissed her again, softly, as I gave her time to adjust to my size. I'd never been with a virgin before, not even when I was one. I'd tried to be as gentle as I could, not wanting to cause her more than pain than necessary. When I felt her body began to relax, I pulled my hips back and slowly sank into her again. She felt fucking incredible, and I wished I could just stay buried inside her. No one had ever gripped my cock the way she did, and she was so fucking wet.

I nipped her shoulder, not hard enough to hurt, but just enough to sting. Her pussy clenched on my cock, and I damn near came. Her hold on me had relaxed, her hands moving to my shoulders, and her legs came around my waist, letting me take her deeper than before. Sweat slicked my skin as I fought for control, not wanting to come before she did. I might not have given her candles and flowers for her first time, but I was sure as fuck going to make her come. I might be an asshole on the best of days, but the woman under me deserved so much more. She hadn't asked for any of this, and I was damn sure going to treat her like a damn princess.

Reaching between our bodies, I flicked my thumb against her clit. Her eyes went wide, and I could see her pulse pounding. Without any other warning, she came with a loud, keening cry, her pussy gripping so damn tight I saw stars. She pulled every drop of cum from my balls as I emptied inside her. Might make me a right bastard that I hadn't even asked before I did it, especially since my sources told me she wasn't on the pill, but the thought of her growing round with my child nearly had me thumping my chest like a caveman.

My lungs were heaving from exertion as I fell to my side, crawling up the bed until my head rested on a pillow. Isabella immediately cuddled against me, her fingers tracing a pattern on my abdomen. She was quiet, but I didn't think it was necessarily a bad thing. After I'd caught my breath, I looked down at her and saw the tender smile on her lips. I hadn't given her soft words, even though I'd tried to be as gentle as I could under the circumstances, and yet she looked completely content.

"Is it always like that?" she asked.

"No," I answered truthfully.

I'd never experienced anything like what we'd just shared. Being with women had always been a quick release for me, but with Isabella, I'd actually felt connected to her. I'd cared whether or not she'd enjoyed it. I'd used club sluts for so long, I'd forgotten what that was like. I'd had steady girlfriends in my younger days, and later in life, some widows who knew the score and hung around long-term, but being with the woman in my arms had been vastly different from any of those experiences. I'd never once been tempted to tie myself to a woman, and I'd not been given much of a choice when it came to Isabella, but I wasn't regretting it. I liked that she was mine. She had my name on her body, would never know another cock other than mine... When I'd tasted her sweet lips three years ago, I'd known no woman would ever compare to her, and I'd been right.

"Think it will always be like that with us?" she asked.

I gave her a smile and smoothed her hair back from her face. "I'm sure it will be."

She deserved more than me. In some ways, I felt sorry for her. I was too damn old to change my ways, and having never been in love with anyone, I wasn't sure I was capable of the emotion. Isabella warranted that, though... love, flowers, dating a guy her age... she'd been denied all that because of her father's demands, but fuck if I wanted to let her go. Even the small taste I'd had of her three years ago, I'd known then I was hanging onto her. She was tiny, barely even reaching my shoulder, but her kisses could take me to my damn knees. It was hard to believe the small woman curled against me could hold so much power over a guy like me, but she did. And if I ever let her know it, I'd be fucked.

"What happens now?" she asked.

"You're going to have to be more specific, baby."

"I don't know what my role is. I know I'm inked as being yours, but I don't understand exactly what that means. Are there duties I need to perform around here? Am I free to get a job outside the club? I don't know what my typical day is supposed to look like."

My arm tightened around her. "You're not a prisoner here, Isabella, but when you leave the compound, there are precautions that will need to be taken. Even though you're mine now, you're still the daughter of Casper VanHorne, which means you're still a target. You will likely always be one, even if your dad were to retire. If you leave for any reason, even to buy groceries, I want you to promise you'll at least take a Prospect with you."

She made a face. "Just not the one manning the gate tonight."

I turned my face to look at her. Fuck if I could remember who was assigned to that post tonight. "What's wrong with the guy at the gate?"

Isabella bit her lip like she wasn't sure she should say whatever was on her mind. But if that asshole had said something to her, I wanted to know.

"It's not entirely his fault," she said. "He didn't know who I was."

"What. Did. He. Say?"

"He wanted me to…" Her cheeks flushed.

Jesus, it was like pulling teeth to get her to talk. "Just tell me."

"He wanted me to suck his cock," she blurted. "But once he saw my tattoo, he backed off."

The urge to go beat the shit out of the guy was a hard one to fight off, but I couldn't go around pummeling every guy in my club. At least he hadn't physically harmed her. My guys were a bit rough around the edges, and if they saw a pretty woman they wanted, they didn't hesitate to go after her. And Isabella was so damn beautiful I knew trouble was going to follow her. The sooner I introduced her to everyone the better. The fact he'd backed off when he'd realized she was mine was the only thing saving his ass right now. That and the fact she said he hadn't touched her. If he'd laid so much as a finger on her, he'd be learning a lesson from my fists.

"I'll make sure everyone knows who you are so it won't happen again," I said. "My men might get upset when I bust their heads every time they flirt with you. And, baby, as sexy as you are, men are going to flirt. I know it's unreasonable for me to think otherwise, but once they know you're mine, they'd better keep their fucking distance."

She smiled a little. "I think I like the caveman routine. But if that guy telling me to suck his cock was his way of flirting, I think they need lessons on how to get a woman more than they need their asses beat."

I snorted but couldn't disagree with her. Assuming they were looking for more than a good time. But most of my guys were content with club sluts. It pissed me off that they'd thought Isabella was one. Just looking at her, you could see the innocence in her eyes. How the fuck they'd missed that I didn't know. Or maybe they hadn't looked past the curves she'd grown over the last few years. She'd been beautiful before, but now she took my fucking breath away. I knew I was a lucky bastard that she was mine, even if she hadn't had a say in the matter. Or me either for that matter. If I hadn't been backed into a corner, I'd have been banging club sluts the last three years and sure as fuck wouldn't have an old lady.

"You need to call your dad in the morning," I said. "And expect a visit from him once he knows you're here."

She groaned and buried her face against me. "Do I have to?"

"Yeah, baby, I'm afraid you do."

"I guess hiding from him for three years is long enough. I know he looked for me."

"He was never going to find you," I said. "I wouldn't let him."

Isabella slowly looked at me. "What does that mean?"

"Honey, I've known where you were this entire time, and I made sure your tracks were covered. If you didn't want to be here, I wasn't going to force the issue. I made sure someone watched over you but kept their distance so you could spread your wings a little."

She blinked, opened her mouth, then snapped it shut.

"I figured you'd come home when you were ready, and if you didn't, I'd have eventually gone after you," I said.

"Thank you," she said softly. "You could have forced me to come back anytime. It was wrong of me to run like that. I was an adult and should have come back like I was supposed to. But thank you for giving me some space."

"I'm not going to keep you under lock and key, Isabella. You want to make friends and go do girly shit with them, I'm not going to keep you from it. But I will protect you at any cost, and if that means someone follows you around town, so be it. And God help anyone who thinks they can take you from me."

"You're a little intense," she said.

She wasn't wrong. At least, not where she was concerned. Just the thought of someone taking her from me was enough to make me go on a rampage. Waiting for her hadn't been easy, but at least I'd known where she was and that she was safe. If someone dared to take her or harm her, they'd answer to me. I'd just have to beat her dad to them, otherwise, he might not leave me much. I'd seen the pictures of what he did to the men who took her before. At least, I'd been assured those were human bodies, but the carnage hadn't left them recognizable as ever having been men. Casper VanHorne was definitely not a man to fuck with. If he ever found out I'd helped his daughter stay off his radar, there would be hell to pay.

"Where's your stuff?" I asked. "You didn't have anything with you at the clubhouse. I should have asked sooner, but I was a little preoccupied."

"It's supposed to be delivered tomorrow. I'll just have to wear my outfit from today until the boxes get here. I shipped everything but what I was wearing. I dropped the boxes at the post office when they first opened with one day-shipping, then caught a ride here."

"If I'd known you were coming, I would have had you escorted, and a Prospect would have hauled your stuff home in the truck."

She shrugged. "I hadn't spoken to you in three years. I didn't know what kind of reception I'd get when I arrived. Honestly, I thought you'd be beyond pissed at me. I was a little scared. I had visions of public punishment in front of your club the entire way here."

I gripped her chin and forced her to look me in the eye. "I will never hurt you. No matter what you do, I could never take my anger out on you. I might yell sometimes, but I will never lay a hand on you when I'm upset, and I won't allow anyone else to either."

"My dad is going to lose it. You know that, right? It's not going to be pretty when he shows up here."

"Your dad has been worried about you. It's understandable that he's upset, but you know he loves you more than anything." I smiled at her. "You just bat those pretty blue eyes at him and give him a hug, and I bet everything will be forgiven."

She snorted. "You obviously don't know my dad very well."

Her stomach rumbled and I smiled, pressing a kiss to her temple. "I'll order us some burgers and get a

Prospect to bring them over. You want fries or onion rings?"

"If I say onion rings, does that mean you won't kiss me again tonight?"

"Baby, even if you had onion breath or morning breath, your lips would still be the sweetest I've ever tasted."

Her cheeks flushed, and I winked at her as I got out of bed. I grabbed my jeans off the floor and pulled my cell phone from the pocket. Calling the clubhouse, I placed our order. Isabella snatched my discarded shirt and pulled it over her head. I had to admit, she looked much better in it than I did. Then again, she'd look sexy as fuck in anything. I walked over to the closet, then reached into the back. I'd had something made for her a while back, thinking she'd come home. My hand closed over the black leather, and I pulled it off the hanger.

I tossed it onto the bed, and Isabella held it up. A smile curved her lips when she saw the *Property of Torch* patch on the front, then turned it over. The back had the Dixie Reapers logo in the middle. The top rocker said Dixie Reapers MC, and the bottom rocker said Property of Torch. She touched the stitching reverently and then slipped it over her shoulders. She fastened the buttons, and my cock got hard as a damn steel post when I saw the swells of her breasts push up over the top. *Fuck me!* I hadn't gotten hard again so fast in a long damn time. Not that I'd ever admit to being old, but I sure as fuck wasn't twenty-something anymore. For that matter, my thirties were a thing of the distant past too.

I pulled my jeans up my legs and carefully zipped them, but left the button undone. The way her hands were caressing the leather was almost enough for me to say fuck the food and crawl back into bed with her, but she was hungry, and I was going to take care of her. With one last look at the tempting woman in my bed, I went downstairs to wait for our dinner.

Isabella brought out tendencies I didn't even know I had. I couldn't remember a time I'd ever been gentle with a woman or gave a fuck about anything other than getting my dick wet. But with her... I shook my head. She was mine, my responsibility, and I was going to give her everything she needed. Maybe not everything she wanted, because there was a difference, but I'd take care of her the best I could. Despite the fact I'd had her watched the last three years, there was still a lot I didn't know about my woman. I looked forward to figuring her out in the days to come.

A knock sounded at the door and I opened it. The Prospect on the other side held out two containers of food. Johnny had been a prospect since he was seventeen. Tank had found him on the streets, digging through the trash for food. The kid had had a hard life and had been living on the streets a few years. He'd been with us two years now, but I'd been waiting for him to mature some more before patching him in. In some ways, he'd grown up too fast, but he still had that lightning-quick temper a lot of young guys had and didn't always know how to control it. I had no doubt the vote would pass when the time came to patch him in. He always did whatever task was handed to him without complaint, and I knew if shit went down, he'd have my back. All things considered, he was a good kid.

"Thanks, Johnny." I took the containers from him. For a kid of nineteen, he was a big bastard. Taller than my six-three, and even wider. He'd packed on some serious muscle since finding a home here. "I'm going to assign some prospects to watch over Isabella when she's not with me. I'd like you to be one of those men."

He stood a little straighter. "I'll protect her with my life."

I fought not to smile. "I know I can count on you, Johnny."

Dismissing him, I closed and locked the door before returning to my room and my woman. She was leaning back against the headboard, her legs crossed. My shirt was so damn big on her it was hiding that sweet pussy of hers. Her hair was tangled around her face from me holding onto it, and her lips were swollen from my kisses. I stood in the doorway a minute, just admiring her. When she saw my appraising gaze, her cheeks flushed. So. Fucking. Adorable.

I stepped over to the bed and climbed onto the mattress next to her, leaning back. I opened the first container and handed it to her when I saw her onion rings inside. She hadn't specified how she wanted her burger, but I remembered my reports saying she had a bad reaction to tomatoes, so I'd told them to leave off the tomatoes and ketchup. Her eyes lit up when she saw the massive burger and what had to be close to twenty damn onion rings. I didn't know where they thought she was going to put all that food as tiny as she was. She bit into her burger, and her eyes closed, an expression of bliss crossing her face.

"When's the last time you ate?" I asked before biting in my burger.

"Breakfast."

I stopped chewing and stared at her, but she seemed oblivious as she inhaled her food. Now I felt like a complete shit that the first thing I'd done when I saw her was drag her home and fuck her, when she'd probably been starving the entire time. Much to my surprise, she finished every damn bite of her food, and it was only then that I realized I never got drinks for us. I fucking sucked at this taking care of someone business.

"I'll run grab us some drinks," I said after swallowing a bite of food.

"I'll get them." Isabella smiled. "If I'm not back in five minutes, send out a search party because I got lost."

I snorted. "The house isn't that damn big."

She flashed her ass at me when she stood up and sauntered out of the room. I didn't think she was doing a sexy walk on purpose, but it was more that she just walked that way. Her hips swished from side to side as she stepped into the hall and disappeared from my sight. She returned a few minutes later with a bottle of beer in one hand and a soda in the other. Isabella handed the beer to me, and I took a long pull from the bottle before setting it aside.

"Thanks, baby. I see you didn't get lost as you'd feared."

She smiled at me as she cracked open the can of soda. "I'll have to explore tomorrow, when it's daylight and I can see everything better."

"We can change anything you don't like. Except my recliner. That stays."

"I wouldn't take your favorite chair from you."

I finished my food and set the container aside, then drained the rest of my beer. It was still early, too early to sleep, and my dick was still hard as fuck. Isabella got up and went into the bathroom. I heard the sink turn on and then silence. When she didn't come back after a few minutes, I got up to investigate and found her staring at her reflection. Her fingers were tracing over the stitching of her cut, but I couldn't read her expression.

Seeing my name across her back was a thing of beauty, though. I came up behind her, bracing a hand on either side of the counter, and nuzzled her neck. She reached up, and her fingers played with my beard. My gaze met hers in the mirror, and the need I saw in those pretty blue eyes had me reaching for the zipper on my jeans. I lowered it with a rasp and pulled out my cock. Isabella's breath hitched, and she leaned forward, her hands on the counter in front of her.

Without a word, I lifted the hem of the shirt she'd borrowed, exposing the most luscious ass I'd ever seen. My cum had dribbled down her thighs and dried on them, and I was more than ready to give her some more. I flattened my hand in the middle of her back and pressed her down so that her breasts pushed against the counter. I could see them in the mirror, spilling out of the top of the cut and peeking through the gaping neck of the shirt.

Her breathing grew harsher as my fingers skimmed the lips of her pussy, finding her wet and ready. I gripped her with both hands, spreading her ass cheeks open and parting that pretty pussy. With a single thrust, I entered her, not stopping until I was balls-deep inside her. Isabella gasped, but her pussy squeezed me, trying to suck me in even more. I didn't know if I wanted to watch her face in the mirror, admire my name across her back, or watch my dick slide in and out of her. I drew back, my shaft shiny from how fucking soaked she was, then I slammed back into her.

"Fuck! You feel incredible, baby," I said, my voice a near growl.

Isabella moaned, and I glanced at the mirror, trying to judge if she was in any pain. The bliss on her face said it was the exact opposite. I watched my cock as I drove into her again and again. That gorgeous pussy of hers was stretched tight around my dick as I powered into her. I fucked her hard, fast, and deep, loving the clasp of her silken walls along my cock. I adjusted my thrusts so that I stroked across her G-spot. It didn't take long before she was screaming out her release, soaking both of us. She whimpered, and I let go, filling her up. My cock jerked with every spurt of cum until I had nothing left to give. Buried inside her, I panted for breath. I could feel my cock pulsing in time with my heartbeat, and I wished I could stay inside her all damn night.

My dick began to soften, and I pulled out of her, watching our mingled fluids slip down her thighs. I helped her off the counter and turned her to face me, brushing her hair back. Cupping the back of her head, I lowered my lips to hers and kissed her, long and deep. When I drew away from her, I started removing her cut and then the shirt before starting the shower. Isabella stepped under the spray, and I kicked off my jeans before joining her.

I didn't have any of that girly soap that women used, but I kind of liked the idea of her smelling like me. I soaped her from head to toe, and she winced as my fingers slid across her pussy.

"Sorry, baby. I shouldn't have been so rough."

"I liked it," she said.

"You're probably going to be sore tomorrow."

She shrugged like it wasn't a big deal, even though I knew it was. Every time she sat tomorrow, she'd be feeling me, where my dick had stretched her wide and fucked her deep. I really was an asshole, especially since I'd gladly do it again if my cock were up for it. Lucky for her, two was my limit for the night. Sometimes getting old was a bitch.

We finished getting cleaned up, then I dried her off. I switched off the bedroom light, and we crawled into bed. Isabella curled up on her side, and I pulled her tight against my chest, her ass snuggled against my cock. With an arm banded around her waist, I closed my eyes and fell into the deepest damn sleep I'd had in for-fucking-ever. Too deep.

Chapter Three

Isabella

My eyes slowly opened the next morning and my vision blurred for a moment. When everything cleared, I realized I was staring at a pair of black tailored pants that were attached to two legs. My gaze drifted upward, stopping on the hands clasping a gun at the man's waist and then farther up the dark red button-down shirt. When I reached the man's face, I groaned and buried my face in the pillow.

"You disappear for three fucking years and can't even call me when you decide to show up again?" He scowled. "I looked everywhere for you."

"I was going to call you today, Daddy. I just got in last night."

"What you should have done, was follow the plan three years ago. But no, you have to run off like a scared little girl. I didn't raise you to shirk your responsibilities."

"Fuck off, Casper," Torch said with a growl behind me. His arm tightened around my waist.

I guess I could be glad that at least I was covered by the sheet. The last thing I wanted was for my daddy to see me naked in bed with a man, even if he had signed me over to that man. I lifted my head out of the pillow and stared up at the man who had taken care of me all my life. To anyone else, Casper VanHorne was a badass killer who got the job done. But for me? He was the man who had protected me, loved me, and made sure I had everything I ever needed. And while most people wouldn't be able to detect it, I saw the hint of hurt in his eyes.

"I'm sorry, Daddy," I said softly. "I know you were worried about me, but I'm fine. I just needed a little time. I'm not running anymore."

He grunted and turned but paused at the door. "Get dressed. I'll take you out for breakfast."

His booted steps echoed down the hall and then clomped down the stairs. I knew it was his way of showing that he'd really left. No way my dad would ever walk that heavy unless it was on purpose. The man could sneak up on anyone. As he'd proven this morning.

"Fuck me," Torch muttered. "Either I'm getting too old for this shit, or the man's a fucking ghost."

I smiled a little. I think Torch had proven last night just how very *not* old he was, taking me not once but twice. Weren't men his age supposed to need a blue pill or something? He didn't seem to have that issue, and I wasn't complaining. The man had a body to die for. Not even the guys I knew who were my age looked as hot as he did. He was just so... big... everywhere. And I did mean *every*where. Not that I had a lot of cocks to compare him to, but I had passed some nude beaches in Europe, and I might have peeked.

Tossing back the covers, I got out of bed, stretching as I stood up. I ached, but in the best of ways. Torch groaned behind me, and I glanced at him over my shoulder. His gaze was glued to my ass. Since he was forming a tent under the sheets, I was going to assume he liked what he saw. And he definitely didn't need any little blue pills. Everything in that department seemed to be working just fine.

All I had to wear were the same clothes I'd arrived in last night. I wrinkled my nose in disgust at the thought of putting them back on. Wearing dirty clothes made me feel gross. But as much as I hated putting on yesterday's panties, there was no way I was wearing those tight ass jeans without any. Talk about chafing in weird places. I was sore enough without digging my jeans out of my crotch all day.

I'd just shimmied into my jeans and put on my bra when I felt hands land on my hips. I leaned back against Torch's chest, and he brushed a kiss against the top of my head. Turning in his arms, I looped my arms around his neck and gave him a good morning kiss. His hard cock pressed against me, and already I was growing damp. I wanted him, but now wasn't the time. I knew that, but it didn't stop me from rubbing against him a little.

"Don't start something you can't finish right now, baby," he murmured against my lips. "Your daddy is waiting downstairs."

I sighed and pulled away, then finished putting my clothes and shoes on. Torch slapped my ass as I walked past him and out the door. Dad hadn't invited him along for breakfast, so I knew he wasn't going with me. When I reached the bottom of the stairs, I found my daddy leaning against the wall by the door, his gun now tucked away, and his arms folded across his chest. Casper VanHorne was an imposing man, and I knew he scared the shit out of a lot of people. But to me, he was just Daddy, and always would be.

"Ready?" he asked, pushing away from the wall.

"You could have at least waited to show up until after my clothes were delivered. I'm having to wear the same thing I wore all day yesterday. You know how much I hate that." I'd leave off the fact that I'd gotten incredibly wet yesterday when Torch had kissed me.

"Guess we're going shopping after breakfast."

"I don't need new clothes, Daddy. The ones coming in the mail will be just fine."

He snorted. "Since when does the mail ever run on time? You'll be lucky if they arrive tomorrow. You should at least let me get a few basics for you."

"Fine," I agreed, knowing it was pointless to argue with him.

When we stepped out of the house, I saw my father's black Lincoln Navigator, and even better, Boris was with him. I flew down the stairs and flung myself into Boris' arms. He laughed and held me tight. I hadn't seen him since my dad had dropped me back off at school after leaving here three years ago. He'd always been like an uncle to me.

"We've missed you, girl," he said with his Russian accent. "Your dad was a right mess when you disappeared."

"Until I realized she'd done it on purpose," her dad said. "Then I was fucking pissed."

I winced. "I didn't mean to worry you, Daddy."

"I should have just left your ass here with Torch the day he inked you. At least then you wouldn't have been able to run, and I'd have known you were safe the last three years."

Boris opened the door, and I slid into the backseat, followed by my dad. The SUV pulled forward and when we reached the gates to the Dixie Reapers' compound, a Prospect opened them up and let us through. Dad didn't say a word the entire trip into town, stayed quiet as we got out at the local pancake place, and only spoke long enough to order his meal when the waitress came over. The silence was worse than him yelling at me.

Our food arrived, and still he hadn't said a word. The tense jaw told me that he was holding onto his temper, but barely. He'd never hurt me, not physically, but when Casper VanHorne was mad at you, you knew it. And it sucked. There was no worse feeling in the world than knowing I'd disappointed my daddy. I managed to eat most of my food before pushing the plate away. He ate his slowly, as if savoring every bite, but I knew better. He just wanted to make me squirm.

"I said I was sorry, Daddy."

His gaze flicked up to mine before he went back to eating.

With a sigh, I settled against the back of the booth and waited.

When he was finished with his meal, he wiped his mouth and placed his hands on the table, palms pressed to the Formica. He stared at me for long moments before sighing and looking out the window.

"I want to be angry with you, but I can't," he said. "I was asking too much of you. You always seemed so grown-up that I thought you could handle being Torch's old lady. I should have known I was pushing you into something you didn't want, even if you hadn't said as much. I know he's too old for you, but I knew he could protect you. We can have the ink removed and find another way. You'll always be in danger."

"I don't want to leave Torch," I said. "I ran because I was scared. Not because I didn't want him, but because I wanted him too much. The way I felt frightened me, and maybe I worried a little that I was trading one iron-tight grip for another. You've watched over my every move for as long as I can remember, and I knew he'd be the same way. Or at least, I thought he would be. I just wanted a taste of freedom. I wanted some time to grow up."

"Fine." His eyes narrowed, and I had a feeling I hadn't heard the end of it. "But if he ever does something that makes you uncomfortable, if you decide this life isn't for you, I'm only a phone call away."

I smiled a little. "I don't think he'd let me go quite that easy."

"Certainly didn't waste any time in claiming you," my dad muttered.

Was that what this was about? He'd thought Torch wouldn't touch me, even though he'd given me to the man? It wasn't like my dad to go back on a deal. Or was something else going on? I had the sinking suspicion that my dad was hiding something, and it couldn't be good.

"He kept his word, you know? He wasn't with anyone the entire time I was gone."

"I know," my dad said.

My eyes narrowed. "What do you mean 'I know'?"

"Got eyes and ears on the inside. That's all you need to know. And it's best if Torch doesn't figure that out."

I snorted. If Torch knew where I'd been but my dad didn't, his eyes and ears weren't doing him too much good. "After you mysteriously showed up this morning, you don't think he's going to find that a little odd? Whoever you have planted, they'll be discovered soon enough."

He shrugged.

"Daddy, I know you mean well, but the last thing I want is for the two of you to end up fighting. I can't choose between you, and I shouldn't have to. Why can't you work together to keep me safe?"

"You're right. We should work together." He rubbed a hand over his face. "There's some stuff going on, Isabella. Stuff I can't talk to you about. But if you're not with me, I want you to stay close to Torch. These men… they won't hesitate to use you to get to me. And it won't be pretty. Last time was a cakewalk compared to what these guys will do."

His words chilled me, and I was wishing that he'd let Torch come with us. I had no doubt that my daddy would try to protect me, but weren't two badasses better than one? He paid for our food and escorted me back to the Navigator, then instructed Boris to take us to the mall. Boris always stayed with the car. I'd once asked my daddy about it, and he'd said it was too easy to plant a bomb. I'd only been about twelve at the time, and that was when I realized that my dad had a lot of enemies, and all the over-the-top security was there for a good reason.

At the mall, Daddy scanned the parking lot before letting me out of the Navigator, and then quickly walked me into the mall. I knew it was a no-gun zone, but he didn't seem to care. He never went anywhere without at least one strapped to him somewhere. And if men were after him, and possibly after me, I hoped he was armed to the teeth and ready to take the assholes down.

Once we were inside, I went straight to Victoria's Secret. If my dad was going to pay for new clothes, I might as well get something pretty to wear for Torch. Casper VanHorne would never dare step foot in such a place, not with his daughter, so he guarded the entrance of the shop. I picked out a handful of bras with matching panties, each of them lacy and feminine. I browsed their sleepwear. As much as I wanted to wear something super sexy for Torch, I knew the clingy scraps of satin would irritate me at night, so I chose a few pairs of boy shorts with matching tanks. While the lady at the register rang everything up, I went and got my dad's credit card from him.

The woman smiled at me as she stuck the sexy scraps into a bag. "That man of yours must take good care of you."

I snickered. "That's my dad out there. And trust me, he doesn't want to know what I'm buying in here. The first time I had to buy a bra, you'd think he was facing a firing squad. He's always waited outside and just handed over his card."

She eyed my dad again, a gleam of interest in her eyes. "Is he single?"

"Uh, probably. But he's defective. He hasn't had a serious relationship since my mom died. Trust me when I say you can do much better."

She sighed. "Isn't that the way it always goes?"

I gave her a small smile, signed the receipt, and grabbed my bags. When I stepped out of the store, I handed the card back to my dad and started leading the way to the next place on my list. He'd said he wanted to buy me a few necessities, but as the bags piled up, he never uttered a word of complaint. Shoes, purses, makeup and perfume, clothes... He carried it all with ease and never so much as flinched at the totals.

I took pity on him around lunchtime. Not to mention I was now starving. Shopping always made me work up an appetite. As we neared the SUV, the rear hatch popped open and lifted. Daddy was loading my things into the back of his SUV when a *pop pop pop* filled the air.

I started to ask if someone was shooting off fireworks, when my dad hit me hard, taking me to the ground. Gravel from the parking lot bit into my palms, and I smacked my head on the bumper of the Navigator. I saw stars for a moment, but they were quickly replaced with a pounding in my head. Boris rounded the car, and before I knew it, he was firing at a car burning rubber through the parking lot. As the engine got louder, I knew they were coming closer. My dad practically threw me into the back of the SUV with my bags and slammed the door shut.

Bullets pinged off the glass and slammed into the car, but I knew if they weren't armor penetrating, they weren't getting through. My dad spared no expense when it came to his vehicles. More gunfire rent the air and I worried that my dad and Boris would be killed. Would those assholes come for me next? If my dad and Boris fell, there would be no one to protect me. Torch didn't have any idea where I was right now, and I had no way to contact him.

Oh, I didn't think the men firing at us would kill me, but there were worse fates for a woman. I could be passed around as their whore or sold to the highest bidder, or both. Bile rose in my throat as everything grew quiet. I peeked through the tinted glass and breathed a sigh of relief when I saw my dad and Boris were still standing and the other car was disappearing at the other end of the parking lot. Dad was holding his arm, though, with blood seeping between his fingers, so I knew he'd been hit.

I climbed over the back of the seat and plopped down onto the leather. I was shaking so bad my teeth rattled. Dad got in beside me, and Boris opened the driver's-side door. Neither spoke a word as the Navigator backed up and hit the road at speeds faster than I was comfortable with. Boris didn't stop for red lights, and he didn't slow down for crosswalks. He was a man on a mission. If the cops had been called, I doubted they could catch up to us. The tires squealed as he pulled into the driveway of the Dixie Reaper's compound, and the Prospect manning the gate barely got it open before Boris was pulling through. Torch stood on the clubhouse porch, his arms folded over his massive chest.

The moment my dad got out and Torch saw the blood, he leaped off the top step and came running. The back door jerked open on my side, and he pulled me into his arms, his hands running over every inch of me. I could see the panicked look in his eyes and knew he was worried that I'd been hurt too.

"I'm fine," I assured him.

He stared at me, and his fingers gently touched my forehead. I winced and he growled. Okay, so maybe I had been hurt, but I hadn't been shot. That was what mattered, right? I wasn't bleeding everywhere, and I hadn't been taken. Those were big positives for me right now.

"It happened when they started shooting at us. Daddy took me to the ground and I banged my head on the Navigator on the way down. I'm fine, really. It probably looks worse than it feels."

"Call Doc," Torch called out to the men gathering on the porch. "Tell him it's a priority."

"Dad got shot," I told him.

Torch narrowed his eyes at me, anger burning in their depths. "I have eyes. You think I give a fuck about him? You could have been killed. Let the bastard bleed for a while."

My dad snorted as he rounded the vehicle, but all it took was one look at my face, and he narrowed his eyes. "Let Doc treat her first. I can wait."

"I think we need to talk," Torch said, glaring at my dad.

My dad nodded and headed into the clubhouse. Torch swung me up into his arms and carried me inside. He didn't stop until he reached a room down the back hall that had his name on the door. He shoved it open with the toe of his boot, then strode inside and eased me down onto the bed. I didn't have any idea why he had a room here if he had a house so close by, but something told me I probably didn't want to know the answer, so I didn't ask. I had no doubt he'd been far from a saint before I came into his life, and this bed had probably seen more action than I was comfortable with.

His fingers traced the curve of my cheek, and he sank onto the chair that was next to the bed. He stared at me as if I might disappear at any moment. I didn't think I would be leaving the compound again anytime soon, unless I was heavily guarded. So much for having a bit of freedom. Whatever shit my dad was mixed up in now had just landed on our doorstep. I wondered if Torch knew what he was signing up for when he agreed to claim me. It was one thing to give your protection to someone in theory, but now that he saw just how much trouble I could be in, I wondered if he regretted it.

"I'm grounded, aren't I?" I asked.

"Oh, yeah, baby. I'm not letting you out of my fucking sight unless you have at least four of my guys watching you. You could have died today. What if that bullet had hit you instead? As high up on your dad's arm as that shot is, it would have gone through your head."

I reached for his hand, giving it a squeeze. I didn't fool myself into thinking the man loved me, but he obviously felt responsible for me. He was worried for my safety. "I'm okay, Connor. Dad protected me. The minute he heard the shots he took me to the ground, and when the car got closer he tossed me into the back of the SUV. It's bulletproof, so I was safe."

"Where did the attack happen?" he asked.

"At the mall. We'd just finished shopping and were coming out with my bags. Dad had put some of them into the back, and before we could get into the SUV, that other car opened fire. I didn't realize what the sound was at first, but Daddy knew right away."

"The fucking mall?" he asked. "Fuck. I thought you were going to breakfast."

"We did. Then Daddy said he'd buy me some new things in case my boxes didn't arrive today. I wanted to call you when everything happened, but I didn't have a way to do that. Even if I'd had a phone with me, I don't know your number. I ditched my burner phone when I came here. I'd planned to get a new one after I was settled."

"I'll get someone to pick up a phone for you today, and I'll make sure you have my number programmed in, as well as my VP's and Enforcer's numbers."

Talk of his VP triggered a memory from the day I first met Torch. "That day... when you inked me. There was a woman here. She said she was with the VP."

He nodded. "That's Ridley. They have a kid who is three now, and they have another on the way. Hell, I'm surprised they haven't had one a year. Venom can't keep his hands off her."

I smiled. "Maybe I can spend some time with Ridley, once things settle down a little. I wouldn't want to bring trouble to her door."

"They live here at the compound. You can visit anytime you want."

A man stepped into the room, his ginger hair streaked with white. The lines around his eyes and mouth suggested he smiled often. He was wearing the same type of cut that Torch had on, and I saw "Doc" stitched on it. I noticed the black bag clutched in his hand and wondered if he really was a doctor.

Torch stood. "She banged her head on the back of Casper's SUV."

"I saw him at the bar with blood running down his arm, but he sent me back here first," the man said. He turned his blue eyes my way. "And you must be Isabella. I'm Doc."

"It's nice to meet you," I murmured.

He sat on the edge of the bed and rummaged in his bag. He pulled out a penlight and checked my eyes. He listened to my heart and ran his fingers along my forehead. When he was finished with his exam, he gave me a kind smile, then stood and faced Torch.

"She seems fine. She's probably going to have a headache. I don't see signs of a concussion, but you know what to watch for. Give her some Tylenol if the pain gets to be too much for her to handle. I don't want to give her anything stronger unless it's absolutely necessary," Doc said.

"You'd better go patch up her daddy. Feel free to put the stitches in without numbing his arm first," Torch said.

I narrowed my eyes at him. "That's mean."

"He put you in danger. It's obvious there's someone after him, and he took you away from here without enough protection. He and that man of his got lucky. Damn lucky. If that had ended any other way, if you'd have been taken, I'd have rained down hell. And Casper knows it too."

I sighed and closed my eyes. I couldn't be angry with him, not when he was just worried about me. I felt Torch's lips brush my cheek, and then his booted steps left the room. The door closed behind him, and I took that as my cue to stay put. I had no doubt he wanted to talk to my dad, and he probably didn't want me anywhere near that conversation. Hell, I wasn't sure I wanted to know what was going on. Maybe the less I knew the better.

I'd stayed safe for three years. Within hours of my dad coming back into my life, I'd ended up injured. I had a feeling it was going to be a long few days, or weeks. However long it took for them to take care of business. I just hoped they did it fast. I didn't really want to venture beyond the fence before it was safe, but being trapped at the compound was going to get old fast, even if I did get to see Ridley again. She'd been sweet to me, and I hoped we could be friends.

My head began pounding, and I curled onto my side. I vaguely remembered something about staying awake when you'd had a head injury, but sleep was pulling me under fast. The last conscious thought I had was that the bed smelled like Torch.

Chapter Four

Torch

"Motherfucker!" My fist slammed onto the table. "Why did you bring this shit here?"

Casper shrugged, then winced and wrapped a hand around his stitches. I hoped they hurt like a bitch. I couldn't believe he'd brought the fucking cartel to my door, to my woman. He'd known they were following him, and still he'd come here. I wanted to kill the asshole. I'd just gotten her back, and now he'd brought those men with him, men who wouldn't hesitate to kill her. I was beyond fucking pissed.

"I wanted to see my daughter," he said.

"I don't give a fuck. She was off their radar. For three fucking years, no one could find her. I doubt they knew she was here until you showed up. I don't care what you have to do, you're going to handle this problem."

Casper's eyes narrowed. "What do you care? You were forced into this anyway. You didn't want to claim her. I should have your property stamp removed and take her home with me."

Rage built inside me, and I knew I was about two seconds from removing Casper's head. I didn't think Isabella would appreciate that, so I held myself back. Barely. Remove my brand from her? Like fucking hell! That woman was mine! She'd been mine for three damn years and no one was taking her from me now.

"You even think of removing Isabella, and you won't have to worry about the cartel coming after you, because I'll be the one to bury your ass," I threatened.

"Fine. Since you feel so strongly about it, she can stay." Casper smirked.

Fucker! He'd done that on purpose, just to see how I'd react, and I'd played right into the asshole's hands. I stared at him and wondered how upset my woman would be if I put another hole in her dear ol' dad. The last thing I wanted to do was upset her, which meant I needed to play nice with Casper. At least for now. I still didn't know enough about their relationship to kick his ass out and bar him from the clubhouse. Isabella didn't need any added stress with this other shit going on now.

And there was the slight chance I'd gotten her pregnant last night.

I'd never thought about having a family, never really wanted one, but the idea of Isabella carrying my child wasn't an unpleasant one. I was getting old, maybe too damn old to start a family, but Isabella didn't seem to mind my age. Hell, I'd taken her twice last night and had been ready for round three this morning, and I hadn't experienced that in a long time. Not that I'd gotten my dick wet the last three years, since I'd kept my word to Casper. Fuck, no one had even come close to making me hard while Isabella was gone. Once I'd tasted her lips, that was it for me.

My loyalty to my crew had never been questioned, and by extension, they hadn't questioned my celibacy while I waited for Isabella to return. As far as my brothers were concerned, she was my woman, and if I'd promised her fidelity, they expected me to honor it. The club might be full of assholes, but once we settled down, we tended not to stray. Not that many of us had an old lady. Doc had been married once, but his wife was long gone. Even though he didn't party much, he was still a favorite of the club sluts. And Venom was so head over heels for Ridley he sneered at any woman who dared touch him.

"I mean it, Casper. Clean this shit up and keep it away from Isabella. I don't care how much you missed her, it was stupid to come here while you had heat on you. What the fuck were you thinking?"

A coldness entered his eyes, and I knew I wasn't looking at Isabella's daddy anymore. I was looking at Casper VanHorne the killer. If he thought it would intimidate me, he was wrong. It wasn't like my hands were clean of blood, and I'd do anything to keep Isabella safe, even if that meant getting into it with her pop. He wouldn't dare touch me on my own turf, not unless he wanted to take down every Dixie Reaper. The man was good, but he wasn't that fucking good. I'd heard about him taking down six men on his own before, but no way he was taking out an entire club. Not without some help anyway, and the man didn't have any friends, except maybe Boris.

"I want you to leave," I told him. "And I want you to stay the fuck away from Isabella until you have everything under control again. I don't care if she calls begging to see you. I don't care that she's your daughter. You brought the fucking cartel to my town, to my club, and to my woman. That shit doesn't fly, Casper. I don't give a flying fuck who the hell you think you are."

His jaw tensed, and I knew he wanted to knock me the fuck out, or at least try. The man made killing look like an art form, but I hadn't survived my shit childhood, eight years in the service, and all the crap this club had been through in the last twenty-five years by being weak. I stared him down, and eventually he backed off. I could tell he didn't want to, though.

"For Isabella's sake, I'll go. And I *will* take care of this. I'll hit them where it hurts the most," Casper said.

My brow furrowed. "It's the fucking cartel, Casper. They don't give a shit about anything but their drugs, whores, and money. Kill their men, or their families, and it will only piss them off, not slow them down. No offense, but killing is more your thing. You may need to call in some people for this one."

Casper snorted. "And just who would I call? I'm not exactly known for being a team player. Yeah, there are guys who owe me some favors, but I need an explosives expert to take out the warehouses of drugs, a world-class hacker to divert all their funds, and a group of men to steal the whores in the brothels they have stashed around the country."

Fuck. Fuck, fuck, fuck. I didn't want this shit anywhere near me or my crew, but he was right. And while he didn't have access to those types of people, I did. But then, he'd known that when he gave Isabella to me. I had the best damn hacker on the planet right down the hall. As for explosives... I was part of a brotherhood before joining the Dixie Reapers, and those men still had my back. They'd come if I called. The whores could be snatched by almost anyone.

"Give me some time to make a few calls," I said. "I'll be in touch."

Casper smirked, gave me a salute, and left. The fuckstick. I hated that motherfucker. Admired him, but hated him.

I ran my hands through my hair and blew out a breath. The last thing I wanted to do was get in the middle of a damn war, but Casper hadn't left me much choice, not if I wanted Isabella to stay safe. I had no doubt he'd thought he could slip past them, see his daughter, then get back out before they realized he was here. The man thought he was God. There was a knock on the door, and I knew my brothers would want to know what the hell was going on.

"Come in," I barked out.

The door opened slowly, and Isabella hesitantly stepped inside. I rose from my chair, intent on picking her up and carrying her right back to bed.

"Baby, you shouldn't be up," I told her.

"I fell asleep, but I think it was only for a few minutes. Someone told me you were in here."

I stepped around the table and walked over to her, pulling her against my body, my arms going around her waist. "I was speaking with your dad. He's brought a lot of trouble with him, the kind that I really didn't want around here. Around you."

She looked at me, worrying her bottom lip with her teeth. "What's going to happen now?"

"Now, I'm going to take you home, and you're going to go right back to bed. You heard what Doc said. You need to rest."

"I didn't see my daddy when I came to find you."

She wasn't going to be happy when I told her why, but it was for her own good. "I told him to stay away from here until this mess is cleaned up. Those men that are after him are really bad news, and they won't hesitate to take you or kill you in order to get to Casper. I know you probably miss him, but for now, he needs to keep away."

"Does that mean I have to stay here at the compound?" she asked.

"I'd feel better if you did, but I don't duet to keep you caged. I promised that you'd have some freedom."

Her hand cupped my cheek. "If I need to stay here for now, I will. Honestly, after what happened at the mall, I'm not in any hurry to go back through the gate and out into the world."

"I'll take you somewhere tomorrow if you're feeling better, but I'm going to take a few men with us. They'll give us some privacy, but they'll be near enough to help if trouble arises."

She laid her head against my chest and that show of trust made me hold her just a little bit tighter. I needed to speak to Wire and get some balls rolling in order to sort out this cartel shit, but right now, my woman needed me. And she'd always come first. I lifted her into my arms and carried her through the clubhouse. I paused on the front porch and stared at my bike. No way in hell I was taking her home on that, not after she'd slammed her head into the bumper of Casper's car.

A Prospect cleared his throat from the other end of the porch. "I can give y'all a ride home in the truck."

"Get the keys."

"Why do you have a truck?" she asked.

"We actually have three. They come in handy when we need to haul stuff, or if someone gets injured and can't ride on the bike. Venom uses one when Ridley is riding with him since she's pregnant."

"Can I go see Ridley tomorrow?" she asked.

"As long as your head's not hurting. I'd rather have Doc check you out once more before you start trying to do too much."

The Prospect came back out, keys in hand, and I carried Isabella to the truck. The Prospect opened the passenger door, allowing me to climb into the truck with Isabella tucked against my chest. The door shut, and she rested against me while the Prospect drove us home. The house wasn't far, and I'd have gladly walked it, carrying her the entire way, rather than put her on the back of my bike while she was injured.

When we got to the house, Isabella pushed open the truck door. I kicked it shut after I got out, then carried her up the steps onto our front porch. Holding her while digging the keys out of my pocket and unlocking the door wasn't quite as easy as it would have been twenty years ago, but I managed. I locked up and went straight upstairs with her. The bed was still unmade from earlier, and I eased her down onto the side of the mattress. Kneeling at her feet, I pulled off her shoes and socks, and slowly undressed her. What I saw when I lifted her shirt, had me cussing.

"Baby, why didn't you say something about your stomach?" I asked.

She glanced down and winced at the scrapes across her belly. "They aren't bad. I think when daddy knocked me down, I must have scraped it on the parking lot."

"Wait here. I'm going to start the shower, then I'm going to help you wash. I'll put some ointment on those scratches when we get out. I know it's still pretty early, but I think you should lie in bed and rest when we're done."

She sighed and looked like she wanted to argue. I took her chin and tilted her face up toward mine.

"No arguments. If you're feeling better tomorrow, I'll take you to see Ridley. You scared the fuck out me today, Isabella. I need you safe, and I need you well. If that means I have to tie your ass to this bed tonight, I'll do it."

"Fine," she said softly. "But I don't like it."

I brushed her lips with mine. "You don't have to like it."

A small smile tipped up the corner of her lips, and she watched as I stripped out of my clothes before going into the bathroom to start the shower. I hadn't lied about her scaring the piss out of me. When Casper had gotten out of the car and I'd seen the blood, my heart had nearly stopped, thinking the worst. That Isabella had made it out of that shit with no more than some scrapes and a bump on the head was pretty damn lucky.

It took me a minute to get the water adjusted just right. I knew if it was too hot, it would probably make her scratches sting like a bitch. I walked back into the bedroom, swung her up into my arms again and carried her into the bathroom. I eased her down onto her feet, my hands braced on her waist until I knew she was steady, and then I ushered her into the shower. I pulled the door shut behind us and let her have the water first. When she was soaked, head to toe, I stepped under the spray and wet myself down, then got busy washing Isabella.

I was as gentle as I could be when I shampooed her hair, knowing she had to have a headache, even if she was acting like she was fine. She tipped her head back under the water, and I helped her rinse the suds out. When her hair was squeaky clean, I slowly soaped the rest of her. Even knowing she was hurt, I couldn't help the fact my cock responded as my hands coasted over her breasts and the curve of her body. Not that I was going to do a damn thing about it. The last thing she needed was me fucking her against the shower wall. Or anywhere tonight for that matter.

I tried thinking of non-sexy things while I finished washing her and managed to get my cock mostly under control. She reached for the soap, but I took it from her. Isabella gave me a cute pout, but I knew if she put her hands on me, I'd be in hell. If she so much as touched my cock, I was going to be harder than a steel post. I lathered quickly, washed my hair and scrubbed my beard, then rinsed off.

There was pain in Isabella's eyes as I shut off the water, and I dried her as carefully as I could, quickly ran a towel over my own hair and body, then set her on the counter and blew her hair dry. I carried her back to the bedroom and laid her down on the bed, then grabbed some ointment from the bathroom drawer and smoothed it over the scratches on her stomach. They didn't look bad enough to require a bandage, and I figured they would heal faster if the air could get to them.

The covers had been kicked to the foot of the bed, and I eased them up over her body, tucking the blankets around her shoulders. I kissed her softly and tucked her hair behind her ear. Walking over to the dresser, I pulled out a pair of boxer briefs and pulled them on before turning the TV on for Isabella and handing her the remote.

"We missed lunch so I'm going to throw something together. We can eat in bed and watch a movie."

"Why am I naked if you aren't?" she asked.

"I try not to answer the door with my dick out. Never know when someone will stop by, and I don't exactly keep clothes downstairs that I could pull on quickly."

"Fine." She sighed. "I think those should come off when you come to bed, though."

I gave her a wink and went to figure out something for us to eat. My kitchen was fairly well-stocked, but I didn't have a lot that could be made quickly. I found a bag of spinach tortellini and a jar of parmesan alfredo sauce. I pulled a pot from the cabinet next to the stove and filled it with water, added a pinch of salt, and turned on the burner. While I waited for the water to boil, I prowled the lower level of the house, double-checking the window locks and back door.

Each house at the compound sat on a large lot, but mine was on three acres. Not that I really needed all that room, or hadn't in the past. If I had kids with Isabella, we'd need a fenced yard. I scratched my beard and wondered if I should go ahead and ask my brothers to put one up for me. There was no guarantee we'd ever have kids. Fuck if I knew if I could even have one. I was fifty-one years old and never once had a pregnancy scare. Of course, I'd always wrapped my dick before fucking anyone, until Isabella, but there were never any guarantees. Nothing was foolproof except abstinence.

I went back to the kitchen to check the water, then tossed in the pasta. I set the timer on the stove for ten minutes and took down some plates, got two forks out of the drawer, then pulled two sodas from the fridge. I not only didn't want her drinking alcohol because of her head injury, I wanted to keep her away from it on the off chance I did get her pregnant last night. I knew it was way too soon to know, and it was a discussion we needed to have. If she said she didn't want kids right now, we'd have to figure something out. Maybe she could go on the pill because I sure as fuck didn't want to use condoms with her.

The timer went off, and I grabbed the colander and strained the tortellini. I dumped the pasta back into the pot, then added the sauce. I turned the burner off, but set the pot back down on it, stirring it while the sauce warmed from the residual heat. I removed the pot from the hot burner and dished up two platefuls before putting the leftovers in the fridge. Pasta was a favorite of mine, so I kept shredded parmesan on hand, and I sprinkled some over both plates.

I placed a fork on each plate, tucked the unopened sodas under my arm, then picked up the plates and carried everything upstairs. I heard the sound of *Titanic* playing when I reached the bedroom and nearly groaned. Just what every man wanted to watch, some chick flick where the guy dies because they can't figure out weight distribution. Yeah, I'd seen the damn thing before. I thought it was stupid as fuck, but women seemed to love the shit out of the damn movie. So if Isabella wanted to watch, I'd suffer through it.

I handed her a plate and a soda before walking around to the other side of the bed. I might have promised to get naked before getting into bed, but it would have to wait until after I ate. I really didn't want burn marks on my dick if a piece of hot pasta fell into my lap while I was eating.

Isabella was so engrossed in the movie, she didn't even notice. After we'd cleaned our plates, I carried the dishes back downstairs, rinsed them, and stuck them in the dishwasher. Before I went back up, I checked all the doors and windows one more time. It wasn't likely anyone would get onto the Dixie Reapers' compound, but I wasn't taking any chances.

Fuck. I needed to text Tank and make sure everyone knew Casper VanHorne wasn't to be allowed back on our property until things were settled. I didn't want that fucker coming back through here to see his daughter until the cartel wasn't up his ass, and despite my conversation with him earlier, I didn't trust him to keep away. I took the stairs two at a time and when I got to the bedroom, I pulled my phone from my discarded jeans. I shot off the message to Tank, then set the phone on the bedside table.

"Underwear," Isabella muttered, even though she hadn't looked away from the TV. I shook my head but stripped off the boxer briefs just the same. I crawled under the blankets and pulled her tight against my side with her head resting on my chest. While we watched the movie, I toyed with the ends of her hair and breathed in her scent. Even though she'd bathed with my soap and shampoo, there was an underlying hint of something that was unique to Isabella. Her hand splayed across my stomach and just the closeness of her had my cock semi-hard. I brushed a kiss across the top of her head.

"How's the head feel, baby?" I asked. "You want some Tylenol?"

"It hurts, but I don't like taking medication."

"There's no point in hurting if you don't have to."

She looked up at him. "What if I'm pregnant? I don't want to take something that could hurt the baby. I know we were only intimate twice, but I'm not taking anything for birth control, and you didn't use a condom either time."

I hadn't thought we'd have this conversation quite in this manner, but since she'd brought it up...

"I should have asked if you wanted kids right now before I took that decision away from you. I know that makes me an asshole, but I can't say I'm sorry. I want a family with you, Bella. I won't lie. I didn't even consider a condom for a second, and I already knew you weren't on birth control. I wanted to fill you with my cum, make you mine."

She smiled a little. "Connor, I knew before I came here what would happen. I already knew you were the type of man to take what you wanted, and I had no illusions that you would ask my permission. I came here ready to be yours in every way."

"So, kids…"

"Will happen when they happen. Maybe you've already knocked me up, maybe you haven't, but I don't want a barrier between us. I liked the way you felt inside me, I liked feeling the warmth of your release. If that means we take a gamble on me getting pregnant right away, then so be it."

I thought about her words for a few minutes while she watched the movie. When she hadn't returned, I'd thought it was because she didn't want to be with me. I was a lot older than her, and I'd thought maybe she wanted someone younger. I'd figured it was an act of rebellion. Then she'd come home and had said she'd just needed some time, had wanted to grow up a little. I could appreciate that, even if it meant I'd lived like a damn monk for three years.

The woman at my side baffled me a little. She was so trusting, so willing to accept that her life was tied to mine. She'd given herself to me last night without a word of protest. The way she curled against me right now, it was almost like she actually wanted to be here with me, as if she'd chosen this all along. I'd expected her to fight, to cry, to tell me how unfair it was that she'd been given no say. But so far, she'd followed my every command without question, had submitted to me completely. I felt like I was missing something. Her father had essentially sold her to me. Well, more of a trade. And yet, she seemed… content.

I never claimed to know everything about women, but something about all this just seemed a little off. The moment I'd seen her picture, I'd known I would agree to Casper's terms. She'd been stunningly gorgeous even at the age of seventeen, and I'm ashamed to admit that I'd gotten hard just looking at that picture. Meeting her in person had made me want her even more. I'd felt like a pervert when my body responded to her. She was definitely all woman now, though. She'd filled out, her face had matured, but there was still an innocence to her eyes. I think that innocence is what called to me the most. I'd never known someone so pure before. Even as a teen, I'd hung around girls who were... well, for lack of a better word, sluts.

I'd thought that claiming Isabella would be a sacrifice, but I was wrong. She made me want to be a better man, for her. Oh, I was still going to curse like a sailor, bust heads, and take care of business. As far as everyone outside his house was concerned, I was still a badass mother-fucker, and always would be. But with her... I didn't want to be that rough guy when I was around her. I'd never be the soft-spoken gentleman that she deserved, but for her, when it was just the two of us, I could try to soften some of my hard edges. Like letting her call me Connor. No one had spoken that name to me since high school. I'd earned the name Torch my first day in the service, and it had carried over into my life here. Very few even knew my real name, and I wanted to keep it that way.

The movie ended, and I noticed Isabella had fallen asleep. I turned off the TV and the bedroom light, then cuddled her close. Her even breaths fanned across my chest, and her hand clutched at my abdomen, as if she were afraid I'd leave if she let go.

"I'm not going anywhere," I whispered before kissing her softly.

She hummed in her sleep and seemed to press even closer to me. I'd never thought about claiming an old lady, but I was glad that Isabella was mine. Having her in my arms, in my bed, felt right. And I knew I'd do anything to keep her here with me.

Chapter Five

Isabella

The sunlight streaming through the bedroom window woke me. Torch was snoring, and I smiled a little. It wasn't one of those loud oh-my-God-the-house-will-fall-down types of snores, but more like the rumblings of a sleepy bear. His lips were slightly parted, and he had an arm tossed carelessly over the top of his pillow. The other arm was wrapped around me, holding me close. I liked waking up like this.

My gaze traveled from his face down his throat to his broad chest. My hand was resting on his abdomen, and the muscles were tight and well-defined under my palm. He had the body of a god. I'd seen twenty-year-old guys who didn't look this good. It was obvious that he took care of himself. The sheet was pushed down to his hips, but I could see the tent that had formed from his hard cock. I'd seen him naked several times now, but I hadn't really had the chance to look my fill. I lowered the sheet, careful not to wake him. The sight of his thick, long cock had me clenching my thighs together.

I kicked the covers the rest of the way off the bed and eased out from under his arm. His legs were splayed, and I crawled between them, sitting on my knees as I admired his body. I ran my hands up his thighs and licked my lips. My gaze flicked up to his face, but he seemed to still be sleeping. Either that, or he was really awesome at faking it. I looked at his cock again. I'd never really thought about a man's dick looking beautiful, but Connor's was. I wet my lips and leaned forward, circling the head with my tongue.

He moaned, but his eyes were still closed. Feeling a little braver, I sucked the tip into my mouth before trying to swallow his entire length. I paused partway down, my mouth full, but his hips flexed and he slid in farther. My eyes watered as he pushed down my throat, but he was pulling away almost immediately. His eyes were open now and focused on me. Connor's hand came up and gripped my hair, urging me down his length again. After the first few strokes I was able to take all of him without my eyes watering. He'd pull my mouth down his cock while thrusting upward, taking complete control. I wasn't sure what it said about me that I got off on him manhandling me like this. I liked it when he told me what to do in the bedroom, or forced his cock down my throat. Maybe it was the fact that I didn't have to think, didn't have to do anything but feel.

Suddenly, he pulled me away.

"Lay on your back, baby," he said.

He got up, and I stretched out across the bed. I didn't know what he wanted, but I'd enjoyed what we'd done in the bedroom so far, so I was going to trust him. He crawled up my body, his legs braced on either side of my torso. That magnificent cock of his was bobbing in front of me, still slick with my saliva.

"Open," he commanded.

My jaw dropped, and he slowly thrust inside my mouth. Connor gripped the headboard as he fucked my mouth.

"That's it, baby, take it all. Let me fuck that gorgeous mouth of yours."

My hands clenched on his thighs, the ache between my legs growing with every stroke. I wanted to feel him in my pussy but couldn't ask for it with my mouth full. The first spurt of cum hit my tongue, and he grunted as he bathed my mouth and throat with his release, his cock thrusting in and out until he was spent. He withdrew from my mouth and moved farther down my body. His taste was salty, but not unpleasant as I licked my lips.

"Spread your legs, baby," he said.

I parted my thighs, and he settled between them, his broad shoulders pushing them farther apart. His mouth latched onto my pussy, and I cried out as pleasure shot through me. He spread the lips and sucked on my clit before thrusting his tongue inside me. His hands curled around my hips, grabbing my ass cheeks and spreading them too. A finger stroked between them, and I gasped, surprised at how good it felt.

His finger played with my back entrance while his mouth did wicked, delicious things to me. He gathered some of my cream on his finger before circling the tight hole some more. I was nearly overwhelmed, not knowing if I wanted to push back against his hand or lift my hips toward his face. My body was tight, and I was already close to coming. He flicked my clit with his tongue just as the tip of his finger eased inside me, and I came, screaming his name. It felt like my body had exploded the pleasure was so intense, but Connor wasn't done.

He continued to lick, suck, and tease my pussy with that sinful mouth of his, while working his finger deeper inside me. I felt completely out of control, my body crying out for more. When his finger started stroking in and out, full, deep thrusts, and he latched onto my clit again, I was helpless to do anything but come again, even harder than before. My body trembled from the force of my release.

Connor was relentless, playing with me until I'd come a third and fourth time. I didn't know how much time had passed, but after my fourth release, he flipped me over and lifted me onto my knees. I felt his cock brush my thigh as he ran his fingers along my pussy. He rubbed my clit in small tight circles; the sensitive bud was throbbing already. I whimpered and pressed back against him. His hand pulled away, and I felt the head of his cock pressing against me, stretching me, and filling me.

"Trust me?" he asked.

"Yes," I said without hesitation.

He leaned across the bed, his cock still buried inside me, and opened the bedside table drawer. He pulled out a bottle of clear liquid, and I heard the lid snick open. Connor spread my ass cheeks, and then the cold stuff hit me. I yelped and he swatted my ass. The sting had me inhaling sharply, and my eyes widened when I felt myself get even wetter.

"You're going to have to relax, baby."

His cock pulsed inside me as I felt him working a finger into my ass again. It had felt incredible when he'd been sucking on me, and even now it felt good. His hips pulled back, then thrust forward as he set up a steady rhythm with his cock. Slow. Deep. I whimpered when he added a second finger to my ass, and it burned at first. His fingers were stroking me in time with his cock, and soon I was pushing back against him, begging for more. I felt completely out of control, and all I knew was that I wanted more. The sensations rolling over me had me seeing stars and gasping as I strained for release.

"Please, don't stop," I begged.

"This ass is so fucking tight. One of these days, I'm going to fuck it."

My pussy clenched, and he growled before fucking me harder.

"Come for me, baby," he said.

I wanted to. Desperately, but my release was just out of reach. I leaned down and laid my cheek against the bed, and the new angle made his cock hit me just right. My pleasure swelled inside me until I thought I was going to break. The fingers in my ass twisted with the next stroke, and I came, so damn hard I could feel my juices running down my thighs. Connor pounded into me harder until I felt the splashes of his hot cum bathing my insides. He growled as he slammed into me twice more, then stayed buried inside me.

He was panting for breath, and if my thighs hadn't been shaking, I'd have wanted to stay like this a little while longer. I felt so full, and so complete. He eased his fingers out of me first, then his cock, before dropping to his side next to me. My legs gave out, and I curled up next to him, not caring that I was covered with sticky stuff from both of us. The scent of sex filled the air, and I breathed it in every time I inhaled.

"I had planned to leave you alone this morning," he said, "but then you were naughty and had to put my cock in your mouth."

I giggled a little and couldn't help but smile.

"I wanted to taste you," I said.

"I'm sorry if I was a little rough. I wanted to go deeper, and I knew that wouldn't happen unless I took over. I get inside you and can't seem to control myself. If I ever hurt you, you have to tell me. I'll stop the second I know you're in pain."

"I don't mind," I admitted. "I like it when you get all commanding with me and take what you want."

He grunted and tightened his arm around me.

"Connor, can I ask you something?"

"You can ask me anything, Bella. Sometimes I may not be able to give you an answer, and sometimes you may not get an answer you like, but I will always be honest with you."

"I know my dad forced you to take me. I heard him talking on the phone about it, and I know I was just a business transaction. Are you sorry that you agreed to claim me three years ago?"

"No," he said. "I'm not sorry. But I have wondered why you agreed to it."

He'd said he would be honest with me, so I owed the same to him. I still felt uncertain around him. Yeah, we'd had sex several times now, and I had a tattoo that claimed I was his property, but we really didn't know a lot about each other. Or at least, I didn't know a lot about him. A man like Connor had probably done a lot of research on me. I doubted he went into anything blind.

"I wasn't given a choice. I was hurt at first, finding out that my dad could just give me away like that, and I wanted to fight him on it. I was scared the day we came here, the day you had me inked. I didn't know what to expect. I figured any man my dad chose would be hard and unforgiving. I expected a bastard who would take what he wanted. But then I saw you and... I don't know. There was something about you that I liked. And when I was getting the tattoo, it was you who calmed me. You didn't have to do that."

"And now? Do you wish that things were different?" he asked.

"No, I like being here with you. The things I felt for you made me feel overwhelmed, and that scared me. I'd never been attracted to someone before, never felt desire. The boys I'd known in school annoyed me more than anything. When you kissed me that day, I didn't want you to stop. The way your lips felt against mine, the feel of your hands on my hips... it awakened something inside me. You were so nice to me, so understanding when you talked to me. And when you kissed me, I wanted more. But I didn't think you felt the same things for me that I was feeling about you. I thought I was just a business deal."

He chuckled a little. "Baby, the minute Wire showed me your picture I got so damn hard my cock was coming out of my pants. I wanted you, but I felt like I shouldn't want you. You were so damn young that I felt like a fucking pervert, but I couldn't seem to control my body or the fact that I wanted you."

"So, you aren't sorry you're stuck with me and can't have other women?" I asked, a little scared to hear the answer. I had no doubt that a man like Connor had been with many women, women who were probably a lot more experienced than me. I knew what happened between the men in the MC and the club sluts. I might be a little naïve at times, but I wasn't stupid.

"I haven't wanted another woman since meeting you." His hand slid down my belly and cupped my mound. "This pussy is the only one I want. It's mine. You're mine. And I'm going to fill you so full of my cum that no one will ever question who you belong to."

I snorted. "Well, you're off to a good start."

I felt his chest shake with laughter.

"Can I go see Ridley today?" I asked.

"Sure, baby. Let's shower and get dressed. I'll call the clubhouse and have someone bring your things over. I'm sure Casper left them before he took off, but I didn't think to check last night."

"It will be nice to have something clean. I can't tell you how nasty it feels to wear the same panties more than once. If my jeans hadn't been so damn tight, I'd have rather gone without any."

Connor groaned and closed his eyes. "Fuck. Now every time I see you, I'm going to be checking for panty lines. If I were twenty years younger, I'd be fucking you nonstop. I swear I just have to hear your voice, and I want you."

"Then maybe it's a good thing you aren't twenty years younger because I don't think I could handle you taking me nonstop. I was sore as hell yesterday, and now today my ass stings too." I kissed his cheek. "But I'm not complaining. I liked what we did this morning."

"I haven't been able to come more than once, that close together, in a long fucking time. I guess you inspire me. You and that tight pussy of yours."

I bit my lip to keep from laughing. I'd always thought my virginity was something of a curse, because all the guys at school had tried so hard to be my first. It had made me the focal point of every bet since high school started, but I was glad that Connor had been my first. Would be my only. As much as I hated to admit it, my dad had made a good choice when he'd picked Connor to take care of me.

Connor reached for his phone on the bedside table and sent off a text. I assumed it was to arrange for my new stuff to be brought over. I knew we both needed to shower. I was excited about seeing Ridley again, but it was kind of nice just lying in bed too. I'd never shared a bed with anyone before, not even another girl at a sleepover. Mostly because I'd never been invited to one. I'd never really gotten along with other girls. I'd found them to be catty and often cruel. But Ridley was Venom's old lady, and since Venom was Connor's VP, I was hoping that meant I would have a new friend. She'd seemed nice the brief moment I'd met her before.

"Go get cleaned up," Connor said, patting my hip.

"You aren't going to join me?"

"Unless you want my fingers somewhere tight and my mouth on you again, then no. I think your body needs a break, especially since I have every intention of fucking you again tonight. I might be old, but even I can get it up again after I've had twelve hours of rest."

I rolled my eyes. "Whatever, Connor. You're not old. Any man who looks as sexy as you cannot call himself old. Old people are fat and hunched over with little to no hair anywhere. Trust me. I passed some nude beaches in Europe. The most hair some of those men and women had were in their noses."

He made a choking sound, then started laughing.

I reached over and cupped his balls. Yeah, they were covered in mostly silver hair, but they in no way looked like the old man balls I'd seen on those beaches. They drew up in my hand as I gently squeezed them.

"When these are naked and hang down to your knees, then you can call yourself an old man." I reached up and caressed his eight-pack. "You can't have these incredible abs and this sexy V and call yourself old."

His gaze heated as he watched me. I reached over and took his hand and placed it between my legs.

"And you wouldn't make me this wet and needy all the time if you were old. So stop saying that. I can't be near you without wanting to feel your hands on me."

He stroked the lips of my pussy before thrusting his fingers inside me. Connor shifted so that I was on my back, and he leaned up on one elbow to peer down at me. His fingers worked my pussy, in and out, slow and deep, while his thumb stroked my clit. He'd already given me so many orgasms I'd lost count and already I could feel another one building. Connor leaned down and pulled one of my nipples between his teeth, giving it a slight bite before sucking on it. I reached up and pulled at my other nipple, my hips thrusting against his fingers.

The doorbell rang, but Connor didn't even hesitate. He kept fucking me, kept teasing me. His beard scraped against my breast as his lips worked my nipple, his tongue flicking against it with rapid strokes. His fingers plunged into me harder and faster, until a loud keening sound escaped me and I was coming again. Connor didn't slow down until the last of the aftershocks had worn off, then he kissed me softly before getting out of bed.

Panting, I watched as he stepped into the bathroom and in the mirror I could see him washing his hands. When he came back, he pulled on his jeans from the night before, zipped them, and headed downstairs. I felt boneless and completely satisfied. If I'd known that sex was this incredible, I might have been tempted to try it before now. But then, maybe it was being with Connor that made it so great.

I stared up at the ceiling and tried to slow my racing heart. While Connor got my new things and brought them upstairs, I decided it would be a good time to get cleaned up. It seemed he really couldn't keep his hands off me, and my body was going to be extremely sore if we played around much more this morning. Theoretically, staying in bed with him all day sounded amazing. But I really wanted to be able to walk normally, and I had a feeling if he played with my nipples too much, wearing a bra wouldn't be much fun either.

While the shower warmed up, I brushed my teeth and untangled my hair. Studying my reflection, I lightly traced my fingers across the beard burn on my breast, and noticed the same marks on my inner thighs. My nipples were still puckered and seemed a little rosier than usual. Probably from Connor's mouth and my pinching. I looked like I'd been thoroughly fucked, and I giggled because that was exactly what had happened. There was a sparkle to my eyes that hadn't been there before I'd come home. Being with Connor seemed to agree with me.

I heard Connor coming up the stairs and the rustle of shopping bags. I turned to face the bedroom just as he stepped inside, both hands full of bags that he set on the floor. There had to be at least twenty there and I wondered if maybe I'd gone a teensy bit overboard. Not like Daddy couldn't afford it, though. When someone hired him for a job, they paid well. I'd once overheard him negotiating a price, and it had been in the millions. I knew my dad was a bad man, and I knew his money was earned the less than legal way, but at least he'd tried to always make sure I had what I needed. Or what he thought I needed.

One thing was for damn sure. If I had kids with Connor, we wouldn't raise them the way Casper VanHorne had raised me. No nannies, no boarding school. I don't recall even having a conversation with my dad until I was about thirteen. I think that was the first time he'd realized that I was growing up, and I wondered if that was the point when he'd decided he'd sell me to the highest bidder. Not that Connor had bid on me. I still didn't know the terms of their agreement, but I knew Daddy had selected Connor to watch over me, and I knew that either a service or money had traded hands.

It didn't matter. Connor wanted me. That's what I would focus on. The things my dad had done, or hadn't done, were in the past. I might be related to Casper VanHorne until the day one of us died, but Connor was my family now. The Dixie Reapers were my family. This might not have been the life that I chose, but it was mine now. I'd always dreamed of growing up and marrying a handsome prince who fell madly in love with me. I smiled a little. Connor was far from princely, but he definitely was handsome. Unlike the pretty boys I'd gone to school with, he was rugged and manly. His fingers were callused and his demeanor sometimes gruff, but there wasn't anything I'd change about him.

I'd only been here for two days, and already I was happier than I had ever been before. I felt like I belonged here, like my place was always supposed to have been by Connor's side. Maybe the Fates had stepped in the day my dad offered Connor a deal. Me in exchange for whatever. Someone, somewhere had obviously been watching over me. I knew the type of men my dad associated with, and most of them left me feeling cold as ice. Their eyes were dead, and if they smiled, it was even scarier than when they didn't.

"What are you thinking?" Connor asked, coming toward me. He placed his hands on my waist and pulled me against his body.

"Just thinking how lucky I am," I answered honestly.

He smiled a little. "Lucky?"

"My dad could have chosen anyone, any of his associates, but he picked you. I could have been given to some Mob boss, or an assassin. Or any other dark and deadly person my father knows. They wouldn't have treated me as well as you do. Getting to be here with you makes me feel lucky, and very grateful." I ran my hands up his forearms to settle on his biceps. "I love waking up with your arms around me. When you hold me close, I feel safe and wanted."

He lifted a hand and placed it against my cheek. "You feel that way because you *are* safe, and you are most certainly wanted."

Connor leaned down and kissed me. It was sweet and tender, and I somehow knew that this was a side of himself he didn't show just anyone. It made me feel special. I liked that he was different with me. Everyone else knew him as Torch, the big, bad Pres of the MC. But with me, he was just Connor. The man who claimed my body and sent me soaring, the man who held me like I mattered. The man who wanted a family with me.

"Your water's going to get cold," he said. "I'll make some room in the closet and dresser for you, but I don't think all this stuff is going to fit. I'll have to get a contractor in here to see if there's a way to expand the closet. If not, there might be room for another dresser or maybe an armoire."

"We can figure it out later. I'll put up my favorite things, and the rest can stay in bags for now."

I kissed him again, then squeezed past him to rummage through the sacks on the floor. I found the one with my toiletries and carried it into the bathroom. The razor,

shower gel, shampoo, and conditioner went into the shower next to Connor's stuff. Then I set my body lotion, perfume, and the handful of cosmetics I'd purchased on the counter. I'd found a really wide brush that I couldn't wait to try out and set it down as well.

Connor came over and stood next to me, peering down at everything. He picked up my tube of lipstick and grimaced. "If you put this on, I won't be able to kiss you."

My eyebrows rose as I stared at him.

"Pink isn't exactly my color," he said.

I bit my lip and smiled. "It's smudge proof. Which means I can drink something, eat something, or kiss you, and it won't rub off."

He grunted, tossed it onto the counter, and walked out. All right. I was learning something new about him already. He apparently didn't like makeup. Or maybe he just didn't like it on me, since I seemed to remember the naked woman on his lap wearing quite a bit of it. I growled as I thought about that skank. I might have been too timid to do anything my first night here, but if it happened again, I wouldn't hide like a coward.

While he worked on the closet issue, I got into the shower and scrubbed my hair and body with my stuff. I'd picked out Eucalyptus-scented things. It had always been my favorite, even though I wasn't quite sure why. I guess something about it soothed me. It had a nice clean smell to it without being flowery and overpowering. I used the razor on my legs and underarms. When I'd gotten my pussy waxed, they'd said it could last anywhere from three to six weeks, which meant I needed to start shopping around to find a place here that could do it for me.

I rinsed and shut off the water. Connor was leaning in the bathroom doorway and my cheeks warmed when I realized he'd been watching me through the glass. He handed me a towel, and I quickly dried off, then started smoothing lotion over my body. Connor inhaled deeply, and a smile kicked up the corner of his lips.

"Whatever you bought, I like it," he said.

When was I finished, I tossed the towel into the hamper and waited for Connor to let me pass. His gaze caressed me head to toe, lingering in his favorite places. He reached out and ran a finger down the slope of my breast before softly pinching my nipple.

"Maybe we should just stay here."

"Why?" I asked.

"Because I like it when you're naked."

I fought not to laugh. "Connor, I can't stay in this house every day, running around naked, just so you can look at me."

"Sounds like a plan to me."

"That's because you're a man. Of course, you'd think it's a great plan. Naked women are probably your favorite thing."

"Not women. Woman."

I was pleased with his answer and gave him a quick kiss before pushing past him. It didn't take long to pull on some clothes, and then I had to sit and wait while Connor showered and got ready. It was tempting to go watch him the way he'd watched me, but I had no doubt he'd tease me if I got caught. So, I waited rather impatiently.

Chapter Six

Torch

I knew Isabella was anxious to see Ridley, but I wasn't taking her anywhere until she'd had something to eat. We'd never discussed whether or not she could cook. I knew her mother had died when she was just a baby, so I didn't think it was likely anyone had taught her. Unless she learned at the fancy boarding school Casper had sent her to, but I didn't think a place like that would teach something like cooking. Didn't all those rich kids come from homes that hired professional chefs?

She traced patterns on the table while I cracked eggs into a bowl. I added a dash of milk and whisked them until they were frothy, then added a pinch of salt, tossed in some diced ham, a handful of shredded cheese, and a bit of finely chopped onion. The medical reports I'd received on Isabella had said she wasn't allergic to anything that could be found in the kitchen. Now whether or not she liked the taste was another matter. I'd studied everything about her over the past three years, wanting to know as much as I could. When she came home, I had wanted to be prepared to properly take care of her. I knew she took her coffee with a heavy dose of mocha creamer, that her favorite ice cream was Baskin-Robbins' World Class Chocolate, that she never painted her fingernails but always had her toenails painted, and when she didn't think anyone was watching she ate raw cookie dough.

Maybe I should have been angry that she'd run off the way she had, but part of me had understood. Even before she'd explained, I'd figured the situation was just too much for her. And I'd gladly given her the space she needed. I'd filled my spare time with learning about her, making sure the people around her could be trusted, and taking care of any problems that arose. And I'd do the same thing all over again if given the chance. Yeah, it had been a rough three years, but we were together now, and that was all that mattered. I liked that she'd come to me because she was ready and not because she'd felt forced to be here.

"Hope omelets are okay," I said as I dumped half the mixture into a well-seasoned cast-iron skillet. "It's one of the few breakfast things I know how to make."

"Sounds great." She smiled a little. "I'm not that good of a cook, but I'm pretty decent at baking. If you get the ingredients for me, I can make just about any type of muffin you want. I'm pretty good with cakes and pies too."

"Where'd you learn to do that?" I asked, looking at her over my shoulder.

"Consuela. Whenever I wasn't at boarding school, she would watch over me at my dad's house. She tried to teach me to cook, but everything either came out raw or overcooked. Baking was about the only thing I could do right."

"I don't mind cooking. I just don't know how to cook very many things. It's why I eat out rather often, or just grab a burger at the clubhouse. I've eaten over at Venom's about once a week for a while now. Pretty much since you left. I think Ridley was worried about me."

Isabella bit her lip. "She's not mad that I didn't come straight home, is she? She seemed really nice when I met her before."

"Ridley doesn't get mad about much, unless you mess with her man or her kid. Fuck with Venom or their daughter, though, and there's nowhere far enough for you to run. She'll find you, and she'll make you pay."

"Do they know we're coming over today?" Isabella asked.

"I texted Venom this morning after my shower. Told him we'd stop by in a little while. I know you'll want some one-on-one time with Ridley, but Venom is very protective of her and their daughter, Farrah. You might be my old lady, but he doesn't know you."

"Does that mean I can't spend time with her?" Isabella asked.

"No, it just means he might stick close for a little while. Don't take it personally. Things have been quiet for Ridley the last three years, but when she came here, she had trouble on her heels. I think sometimes Venom worries she could still be taken from him."

"Three years ago? That's the favor my dad gave you, isn't it? You took me in exchange for him handling whatever was going on with Ridley."

I nodded. No sense in lying to her. There was a chance that Ridley would say something at some point. It had taken me damn near a year to get Ridley to stop thanking me, and I didn't miss the looks she cast my way when Isabella didn't show up like she was supposed to. Ridley always felt like she owed Isabella something, and owed me. To her, we'd sacrificed ourselves so she could remain safe. In all honesty, I was glad that Isabella was mine, regardless of how I got her. At first, the idea of claiming her had pissed me off, even sickened me a little since she was so young. Until I saw her. Even the tiny-ass picture on Wire's phone had gotten me hard as a damn post. All it had taken was one look, and I knew she was going to be mine.

I dished her omelet out of the skillet and plated it. I set it on the table in front of her and gave her a glass of juice before starting my own breakfast. I pulled out a jalapeno pepper, diced it up small, and tossed it into the bowl, then added some green bell pepper. I'd left them out of hers since I didn't know if she liked spicy food. Isabella ate quietly while I fixed my omelet. I dumped some salsa over it, and by the time I joined her, she was almost finished.

"This was really good," she said.

"When I was in the service, there was this guy who loved to cook. Didn't really get much of a chance where we were, but he talked about food all the damn time. He'd explain in detail how to make all these different dishes, and talked about textures and stuff. I didn't get half of what he was saying, but I guess some of it stuck. I took the things I remembered and learned how to make some basic meals. It beat eating crap out of a box all the time."

"What branch of the service were you in?" she asked.

I didn't talk about my days in the military, but then, Isabella wasn't just anyone. She was mine, and if she wanted to learn more about me, the least I could do was tell her. Well, tell her some of it anyway. I'd done things for my country that I couldn't disclose. But I could give her the basics.

"I joined the Navy when I was seventeen. Went through boot camp, then went through BUD/S."

Her brow wrinkled. "What's that?"

"I went through training to be a Navy SEAL."

Her eyes widened, and her mouth dropped a little. "You were a Navy SEAL?"

I nodded and ate my breakfast. She stared at me for a few minutes and I could tell she had more questions. Women had always thrown themselves at me when I'd been on active duty, and even after, once they learned about that. Isabella, though... while she'd looked surprised, I don't think it had the same effect on her. For whatever reason, she seemed hesitant to ask questions of me. With her, I was an open book. As long as the information wasn't classified, I'd share it with her. She got up and carried her empty plate to the sink, where she rinsed it, then stuck it in the dishwasher. She did the same with her glass once she'd finished her juice, then sat back down.

"Why did your parents agree to let you enter the Navy at such a young age? Don't you need permission to sign up before you're eighteen?"

"Probably best if you don't know how I managed that. As to my parents... I have no idea who my dad is. My mom had a never-ending string of boyfriends who liked to beat the shit out of me, when they weren't too busy selling her to pay for their drugs. For all I know, my dad was some random guy off the street who paid to fuck her. She was hooked on heroin, among other things. But as bad as shit was at home, I know it could have been worse. At least the men in her life only beat on me. I found ways to keep myself fed, even when they used all the grocery money on their bad habits, and I stayed in school. I was barely passing and knew that my best way out of that shit hole was the military. We not only lived in the worst part of town, but we lived in the most rundown building there too. It wasn't uncommon for kids or teens to go missing."

There wasn't pity in her eyes, which was good. I fucking hated it when people pitied me. But there was compassion there. Isabella had lived a very different life from mine. She'd been given every material thing she could have possibly needed or wanted, lived in a mansion, went to boarding schools... but I sometimes wondered if maybe the thing she'd been lacking was love. There was no doubt her father cared about her, but I didn't think he knew how to show it all the time. Or maybe he just didn't want to. I remembered the day I'd had her inked. He hadn't soothed her fears in the slightest. I'd been the one to hold her hand and speak softly to her. I didn't know if Casper planned it that way, or if he just hadn't given a shit that his kid was crying.

I pushed my plate away and reached for her hand, lacing our fingers together in the middle of the table. "I know I'm not perfect, I'm not even a good man most days. But I promise that I'll take care of you, and if we have kids I'll take care of them too. You'll never go hungry. You'll never have to worry about me selling you to someone. I will protect you with my last breath. I may have come from a shit background, and there's blood on my hands, but you never have anything to fear from me."

"You've never scared me, Connor. Oh, I might have worried about how you'd react when I finally came home, but even then I didn't think you'd really hurt me. How I feel about you, though, that scares the shit out of me."

My lips twitched. It was good that she wasn't scared of me, in the sense she thought I'd hurt her. I'd like to know more about those feelings of hers, though. The way she wouldn't meet my gaze told me she wasn't ready to talk about it just yet. I'd give her time. It wasn't like I was going anywhere, and neither was she. I cleaned off my plate and put my dishes in the dishwasher. I glanced at the clock on the microwave and hoped Venom had had enough time to get Ridley and Farrah ready for a visit. I didn't think I could hold Isabella off much longer.

She stood, and I swept my gaze over her from head to toe. She'd pulled her hair up in some sort of loose knot on top of her head, but a few pieces had escaped. The shirt she'd chosen was ruby red and hugged her breasts like a second skin. The jeans encasing her amazing legs looked painted on, and she had on those sexy boots that made me want to fuck her, but it was the cut with my property patch on it that looked the best on her.

"Can we go now?" she asked.

"Yeah." I pushed my chair back and stood, stretching until my back cracked. "We can go. Since I left my bike in front of the clubhouse, we'll have to walk over and get it before going to Venom's. His house is a little farther back in the compound. I don't think you want to walk that far."

"I don't mind the walk, but I will gladly ride on the back of your bike."

I followed Isabella through the house and out onto the porch, then locked up behind us. Her hand slipped into mine as we walked toward the clubhouse. I couldn't remember holding hands with a woman. Maybe in high school I might have a time or two, but no one had tried since. I liked the feel of her hand in mine. It was small and soft, dainty like the rest of her. She barely reached my shoulder, and even with her curves, she was still slight. Isabella reminded me a little of a pixie. If this morning was any indication, she was mischievous like one. Not that I minded waking up to her sucking my cock.

When we reached the clubhouse, my bike was right where I left it. I climbed on and helped Isabella onto the back before twisting the key in the ignition.

The bike roared to life, and I turned the throttle, revving it a few times. Isabella clutched at my waist as I walked the bike backward, then took off out of the parking lot. The road through the compound curved all over the place. It didn't take me long to learn that if I accelerated into the turns, Isabella would squeeze me a little tighter. I might have done it on purpose a few -- dozen -- times.

Venom was on his front porch when we pulled up, leaning against a post with his arms folded over his chest and his ankles crossed. His gaze went from me to Isabella, and I knew he didn't know what to make of her. We'd talked about her a lot since the day I'd claimed her, and I knew Venom had grown skeptical that she'd ever return. He thought she'd screwed me over, and because of that, he wasn't her biggest fan. As far as he was concerned, she should have brought her ass home when she was supposed to have been here. The fact she had run made her untrustworthy in his eyes.

"Glad you decided to show up, Isabella," he said, his voice gruff and unforgiving.

"Play nice, Venom."

He stared at her hard, and she held onto me a little tighter. I patted her hands so she'd let go, then got off the bike. She remained on the bitch seat staring at my VP like he was a demon straight from hell. In her defense, Venom was a rather intimidating bastard when he wanted to be, especially with his beard bushier than usual. The fact that his dark gaze was pinning her in place probably didn't help.

"Back. Off," I growled at him and narrowed my eyes.

His gaze jerked to me, then he pushed off the post and headed inside. I shook my head and offered a hand to Isabella. She got off the bike slowly, not looking away from the door Venom had just stalked through. I could feel the apprehension rolling off her in waves. Venom would loosen up once he realized she was here for good. I knew my VP pretty damn well, and while he was protective of his family, that protection extended to his MC brothers too. He was worried about me, thinking Isabella was going to fuck me over, but I was a big boy and could take care of myself. If he said something to upset her, though, I might have to put my fist through his face.

Isabella followed me up the steps and into the house. I could feel the heat of her body as she stayed close to me. Cartoons were playing in the living room, so I headed in that direction. Farrah was on the floor sitting amongst a mountain of pillows and blankets watching some cartoon with kids who looked like superheroes. Ridley was leaned back on the couch, the lower part of her pregnant belly showing as her shirt rode up a bit.

Ridley smiled so big I thought her face might crack as she huffed and puffed her way up off the couch, then hurried over to Isabella. I had to admit she was pretty darn cute when she waddled around. Ridley shoved me out of the way so she could wrap her arms around my woman, and I chuckled as I stood back and watched them.

"You're here!" Ridley squealed. "I knew you'd come back."

Isabella's eyes closed a moment as she hugged Ridley. I felt Venom's presence and looked over. He was staring at the women, but he had a half-smile on his face. If Ridley was happy Isabella was here, then Venom was happy. Or as happy as he was going to get anyway. He loved Ridley more than life itself, and tried to give her everything she wanted. So if Ridley wanted Isabella to come visit every day, then I knew Venom would allow it.

"I'm sorry I was gone for so long," Isabella said as Ridley pulled back.

Ridley waved her off. "I'm sure you had your reasons. I knew you'd eventually get here."

Isabella looked confused. "How did you know?"

"Because of the way you looked at Torch," Ridley said, grinning ear to ear. "It was the same way I look at chocolate when I'm PMS-ing. Like he was the greatest thing since sliced bread. I knew from that one look that you were hooked."

Isabella blushed and glanced my way before turning back to Ridley. She motioned toward Ridley's stomach. "How far along are you?"

"About seven months," Ridley said. "I don't understand counting things in weeks. Drives me nuts trying to keep track of it. We're having another girl."

Isabella leaned a little closer and whispered loud enough for me to hear. "You know, I've heard that if you have a girl, it means your husband came before you did. Maybe you should talk to Venom about making sure you get there first so you can have a boy next time."

Venom glared at her, and I couldn't hold back my laughter. I never would have expected anything like that to come out of her mouth. Venom growled and stalked over to the women, pulling Ridley into his arms. He kissed her hard and deep before narrowing his eyes at Isabella.

"I please my woman just fine."

Isabella gave him an innocent look, but I could see the laughter in her eyes. "I swear it's true! You can look it up. There are articles about the female orgasm and the gender of the baby."

"Stop teasing him," I said. "You're going to give the man a complex. Now poor Ridley won't get any rest because he'll feel he has to prove she comes before he does."

Ridley winked. "I'm not complaining. I might be the size of a house, but my hormones are out of control. I could have sex at the drop of a hat these days."

"Please don't," Isabella said. "If your clothes start coming off, I'm leaving."

Ridley snickered and grabbed Isabella's hand, leading her over to the couch. Farrah had yet to even look up from the TV. Whatever she was watching seemed to fascinate her. I stood next to Venom, watching the women. Ridley was a few years older than Isabella, but it looked like they were going to be good friends. I think Ridley had decided she was going to like Isabella from the beginning. While Venom made sure Ridley had everything she needed, the majority of the females at the clubhouse were club sluts, so she didn't really have any friends. Not inside the compound anyway. A handful of members had old ladies, but none as young as Ridley and Isabella.

"You did this on purpose," Venom said softly.

"Did what on purpose?"

"Brought her here. You knew Ridley would be happy to see her, and now I'm going to have to be nice to the bitch, even after what she did to you."

I studied Venom a moment and gathered my thoughts so I wouldn't say or do something I might regret later.

"I've known where she was the entire time," I said. "I could have gone after her, but I didn't. She had her reasons for staying away, and that's as much as you're going to get from me. I'm happy she's here, Ridley's happy she's here, so I'd appreciate it if you'd welcome her and stop giving her pissed-off looks."

Venom sighed. "Fine. You know, when she first came here, I thought maybe she'd be good for you. I knew you were just taking her as your old lady to protect Ridley, and I appreciated that more than you can know, but my woman is right. Isabella looked at you like you'd hung the moon, and the heat in your eyes when you saw her made me think maybe things would be okay between you two. But when she didn't come back, I figured I'd been wrong."

"You weren't wrong, Venom. She just needed some time. Time that I was happy to give her. But she's here now. And she might be in some trouble."

His gaze sharpened. "Trouble?"

"Casper VanHorne somehow found out his daughter was back, which is something we need to look into. I think we have a rat on her daddy's payroll. Casper showed up yesterday morning, but he's brought some friends with him. The cartel is on his ass. They shot at him while he was out shopping with Isabella."

"Is that why she's all bruised up?" Venom asked.

"The bruise on her cheek is from a Prospect, but he's been dealt with. The one on her forehead is from yesterday. Her dad tackled her to the ground when the shots rang out, and she banged her head on the car."

"And you think the cartel might be after her now?"

"I don't know. If they know she's Casper's daughter, it's possible they might try to get her to use as leverage against him. I have a plan, though. I was going to let Casper clean up his own mess, but killing is more his style. A bloodbath won't solve anything with the cartel, not unless he wipes out every single fucker. I need you to call Rocky."

Venom's eyebrows shot up. "You know he's been playing the part of a recluse on that damn mountain of his in Colorado. Whatever he was doing for the military fucked him up."

"Yeah, but I need someone good with explosives. Tell him to gather a team. I'm going have Wire send him some files, places that I want taken out. I need it done sooner rather than later. Tell him to use whatever resources he needs. I'm sure VanHorne will be happy to foot the bill."

"You're going to blow up their warehouses, aren't you?" Venom asked.

"Among other things. I'll have Wire hack into their accounts and divert their funds elsewhere. If they have no product and no money, they won't be able to do as much damage."

"They don't just deal in drugs and arms."

I smiled. "That's why I want another team to take out their whorehouses. Get the women to safety. I want every damn one of them cleaned out."

Venom whistled low. "That's going to take some serious manpower. We're talking multiple locations both here and out of the country. How the hell are you going to pull off something that big?"

"I'm going to make some calls." It was time to call in some favors. Starting with the Irish Mob. I knew O'Shay would help, no questions asked. The man wouldn't still be breathing if it wasn't for me, him or his family. Fucker owed me big. Besides, I had a feeling he'd want in on this anyway. Pretty much everyone hated the fucking cartel.

"Whatever you need, I'm there. If it weren't for you and Isabella, my Ridley could be dead right now, or sold to some asshole overseas as a sex slave."

My phone rang, and I saw Casper's name on the screen. I tilted my head toward the front door, and Venom and I stepped outside. When the door shut behind us, I answered the call and put him on speaker.

"I'm taking care of it," Casper said.

I glanced at Venom. "You're taking care of what?"

"I'm guaranteeing the cartel will stay the hell away from my daughter. You can call off your boys. I won't be needing your help after all," Casper said.

Venom's brows lowered, and he gave me a "what the fuck" look. I was just as stumped as he was. Unless VanHorne had figured out how to kill every member of the cartel and their families in the last twenty-four hours, how the fuck did he have it handled?

"Casper, where are you?"

"At a chapel in a quaint little town in Mexico."

"A chapel?" I asked.

"Where else would I get married?" Casper asked.

Married? I stared at Venom, and he looked as surprised as I was. Who the fuck was VanHorne marrying? The man was known for having a string of mistresses, but he'd only ever said vows to one woman. Isabella's mother. I didn't know how my woman was going to handle the news.

"It's not a love match, and my new wife is aware of that. But she'll be taken care of, and that's more than I can say for what would have happened to her if I hadn't intervened," Casper said.

"Quit being so fucking cryptic," Venom said. "Tell us what the fuck is going on."

"To put it in simple terms, Miguel Juarez had a little problem in the form of an illegitimate daughter. In exchange for me taking her off his hands, and promising that she will never again step foot in Mexico, he's calling off his men."

"So you married her?" Venom asked slowly. "Does she have a magic pussy or something?"

My phone dinged, and I pulled up the picture Casper had sent. My eyebrows nearly climbed into my hairline. The woman looked to be near Isabella's age, and wore a body-hugging white lace dress that showed off every curve. She had what I'd always heard referred to as child-birthing hips, and her breasts nearly spilled out of their confines. She was attractive, and the smirk she was aiming at the camera combined with the sultry look in her eyes answered Venom's question well enough.

"And you're certain this means my woman is safe?" I asked. "Because if I set her loose on the town and some cartel fuck comes along and snatches her, you're going to be the one I come after first."

Casper chuckled. "I have a signed contract. In exchange for me taking Carmella, he will leave me and my family alone, and by extension that means they won't fuck with you either."

"Well, that's rather anticlimactic," Venom muttered. "But it's better than waging all-out war."

I heard her say something in Spanish, and her voice sounded like smooth whiskey. Yeah, Casper was going to have his hands full with that one. And just wait until Isabella found out her stepmother was around her age. I could only imagine how that was going to go down. My sweet woman might be mild-mannered from what I'd seen so far, but I wouldn't put it past her to let her daddy know exactly what she thought about Carmella.

"My wife says that she would love to meet you sometime and that you and Isabella are welcome at our home any time you wish," Casper said.

"Uh-huh," I said. "I'll be sure to let Isabella know that your wife of two minutes was kind enough to invite to visit her dad in the house she grew up in. Tell me, Casper, how well do you think that will go over?"

"Perhaps it's best if they don't meet just yet," he said. "Or ever."

"I'll try to explain things to her," I said.

He sighed. "Won't matter. She'll feel like I'm betraying her mother. When my wife died, I swore I would never marry again. And I've kept that vow all these years, but this was the only way I knew to make sure the cartel stayed away from my daughter. You were right. I should have never come to see her until I had things handled. She may be yours now, but it was my responsibility to take care of this, so I did. Hopefully she'll be able to understand that one day."

Carmella said something else, and Casper chuckled.

"My new bride is reminding me that I promised her father we'd be out of Mexico tonight, so I need to go. Tell Isabella that I will call her soon. For now, it's probably best if I come visit her there, or we meet somewhere neutral."

"Congratulations on your marriage, Casper," I said. "Just do me a favor. Don't have any more kids until Isabella has at least one."

"No worries there. We won't be having children at all."

The woman said something else and sounded pissed-off. I had a feeling he'd omitted that part before he married her. Before the phone disconnected, I heard him yelling back at her in rapid Spanish. Well, that was going to be a fun honeymoon.

"So, just how pissed is your woman going to be?" Venom asked.

"I'm not sure I want to find out."

He nodded, and we went back inside. Farrah had moved to Isabella's lap, and the sight of her holding the little girl did funny things to me. She looked so happy as she talked to Ridley, while Farrah cuddled against her chest.

Venom looked from me to Isabella and chuckled.

"What?" I asked.

"I saw that look. The one that says you want to haul her out of here and start the baby-making process. You sure an old man like you can handle some rug rats running around?"

I punched him on the arm. "Asshole. Isabella has assured me I'm not old."

He smirked but didn't say anything else. If I didn't know he was joking, I'd have kicked his ass for calling me old. It was one thing for me to do it myself and another for someone else to say it. We stood in the doorway, watching our women, until Ridley decided it was time to eat.

"I want Chinese," Ridley said, coming to stand in front of Venom, her hand on her hip. "Your baby is demanding lo mein. And sweet and sour chicken. Maybe some shrimp fried rice and a few egg rolls. Oh! And egg drop soup, with wontons."

Venom rubbed a hand over his beard. "Want me to bring it here?"

If I weren't used to the massive amounts of food Ridley consumed when she was pregnant, I might have been surprised at her demands. But when she'd been about this far along with Farrah, I'd watched her eat two large pizzas all by herself, then she had a slice of cake almost the size of her plate.

Farrah toddled over and grabbed her daddy's leg. Venom picked her up, kissed her cheek, and waited for Ridley to decide what she wanted to do. Isabella came to me, wrapping an arm around my waist.

"You hungry too?" I asked.

"I could eat. Maybe not as much as Ridley, but yeah, I'm hungry."

Venom snorted. "That's because an elephant isn't as hungry as my woman when she's pregnant."

Ridley stomped on his foot, and Venom winced.

Pointing to her belly, she growled at him. "Do you see this? *You* did this to me. I'm incubating a human for you, so you'd better damn well feed me whatever I want when I want it. If I want Chinese food, the real stuff from China, then you'd better figure out how to get it to me."

Venom rolled his eyes. "Are we all going or am I picking it up?" he asked again.

Ridley crossed her arms over the top of her rounded stomach. "I want to go, but I don't want to change clothes first."

"I think your yoga pants and T-shirt are cute," Isabella said. "No one will say anything to you if you go out dressed like that."

I kissed her cheek, thankful she was trying to calm Ridley down.

Ridley smiled at her. "I knew I liked you."

"Fine. I'll take you and Farrah in the truck, but I don't think Torch and Isabella want to be crammed into the backseat with Farrah's car seat."

"We'll take my bike," I said. "Chang's over on Fifth?"

Venom nodded.

While he loaded his family into the truck, Isabella and I took off on the bike. We only owned a few trucks, and since Venom was currently using one for his family, I knew we'd have to make some changes. My VP wasn't hurting for money, so I'd let him know he needed to start shopping for something more permanent for Ridley and the girls. And now that I knew Isabella was safe, I planned to seriously start working on a baby. Which meant I needed another vehicle too.

I'd always hated riding anything but my bike. But I somehow didn't think I'd mind so much if the beautiful woman I'd claimed was next to me, and our little one growing inside her. No, I didn't think I'd mind that one little bit.

Chapter Seven

Isabella

Standing at the kitchen sink, I sipped my juice and looked out the small window. The sun was shining brightly, and the clock on the microwave said it was nearly nine. Connor had somehow managed to slip out of bed and leave the house without me hearing a thing. I'd woken to find his side of the bed cold, and I'd hugged his pillow close and closed my eyes a few more minutes. I'd been more tired than usual the last few days, but my breasts ached too so I figured my period was coming. It was a little late. Two weeks late, to be precise, but I'd never been all that regular. The stress in my life always had my body screwed up. But I didn't have much to be stressed about right now.

Connor had assured me the issue with the cartel had been handled, even though he wouldn't tell me what he'd done. When we'd come home from Ridley's three weeks ago, he'd told me that I was safe. Just that morning he'd been worried, so I hadn't believed him at first. The cartel didn't just back down for no reason, after all. But then he'd called my dad, and Daddy had confirmed it too. Daddy had sounded off, and had hung up quickly, which wasn't like him unless he was on a job. And I didn't think he was on a job. I could have sworn I heard a woman in the background, but hadn't really thought much of it. I knew my dad wasn't exactly celibate, even if he had said he would never marry again. At sixty-two, he hardly had one foot in the grave. Although I tried really hard not to think about my dad having sex. That was just gross. Babies were supposed to come from the stork and not because your parents got naked.

Despite the assurance that I was safe, Connor still wanted at least one Prospect to go with me if I left the compound. Most times, it was Johnny who was assigned to me. He was just a year younger than me, and we got along really well. Even though I knew he had to hate going to the mall or hanging around outside the salon, he went wherever I did without complaint. There was a watchfulness to Johnny that made me feel safe with him. He was always scanning the area, looking for trouble, and I was never allowed to enter anywhere unless he'd checked it out first. Even the ladies' bathroom, which had embarrassed me to no end at first. If he weren't part of an outlaw club, he probably would have made a good cop. Those two definitely didn't mix, though.

I didn't really understand how the club worked. I knew they had to be doing something for money, and since Connor had just bought me a brand-new SUV, it had to pay well. I wasn't certain I wanted the details, though. If I found out they owned whorehouses or something, I might lose it. My dad earned a less than honest living, but selling women or giving drugs to kids really bothered me. I knew whatever Connor was doing wasn't legal. I might be a little naïve sometimes, but I wasn't stupid. My dad didn't exactly deal with law-abiding citizens. That he chose Connor for his only daughter told me plenty.

I took another swallow of juice, but my stomach suddenly pitched and rolled. My eyes widened as the glass slipped from my hand, bouncing off the counter and shattered across the floor as juice went everywhere. I jumped back, a piece of glass slicing into the sole of my foot, and went running for the downstairs bathroom. My knees had barely hit the floor before I was hunched over the toilet puking up everything I'd eaten that morning. I heard pounding on the front door, but couldn't get up to answer it. My stomach heaved again, and again, until nothing was left to come up. Tears blurred my eyes as I curled up in the corner of the bathroom, my hand over my tummy.

There was more pounding at the door, but I was scared if I got up, my stomach wouldn't be happy with me. After several minutes of silence, I heard the front door crash open, and Connor was yelling my name.

"Isabella!"

"In here," I yelled back.

I heard him cursing as he came toward me. He paused in the bathroom doorway before coming forward and kneeling in front of me. His gaze was concerned as he reached over and ran a finger down my cheek.

"What's wrong, baby? And why the hell are there bloody footprints in the hall?"

I winced. "I cut my foot when I dropped the orange juice glass. I was standing at the kitchen sink when I suddenly felt like I was going to throw up. Which I did several times when I got in here."

He pressed the backs of his fingers to my forehead. "No fever."

"Maybe I have a stomach bug. I've been a little tired lately."

Connor closed the toilet, flushed it, then sat on the lid. He reached for my feet, inspecting first one and then the other.

"Where were you?" I asked.

"I called Church this morning. Then Johnny called my cell and said you weren't answering the door, so I got worried and came to check on you."

"I didn't mean to worry you. He started knocking right about the time I had to run in here. I was scared to move afterward, in case it upset my stomach again."

Connor leaned over and pulled out a kit from under the sink. He snapped the lid open and took out a large bandage and ointment, along with an alcohol wipe. I knew that was going to sting like a bitch. He picked up my injured foot again, cleaned the wound, then put the ointment and bandage on it.

"It doesn't look that deep, but it's a pretty long cut," Connor said. "Might hurt to walk until it heals."

Connor stood and lifted me into his arms. He set me on the counter and handed me some mouthwash. I was more than happy to get rid of the nasty taste in my mouth, then he carried me out of the bathroom and toward the front door. Johnny was leaning against the wall, and looked worried when he saw me in Connor's arms.

"I'm okay," I assured him.

"You're not okay. You're going to the doctor," Connor said.

"But…"

His glare silenced me.

"Get her shoes by the back door," Connor told Johnny. "Then meet us at the Expedition."

Johnny nodded and took off toward the back of the house while Connor carried me out to the SUV and settled me on the passenger seat. He fastened the seatbelt across me, then kissed my lips softly.

"I think you took ten years off my life when Johnny said you wouldn't answer the door."

"I'm sorry."

Connor cupped my cheek and kissed me again. "We're going to get you checked out. Doc's good to have around for an emergency, but I want to take you into town to see Doctor Myron. He's Ridley's doctor."

My brow furrowed. "Her OB-GYN?"

Connor didn't say anything and just stared at me.

"Wait, you think I'm pregnant?" I asked.

"Bella, I've taken you in the bed, on the dresser, in the shower, against the kitchen counter... every time my dick's been hard, I've bent you over and claimed your pussy, filling you up with my cum. It's not unreasonable to think you might be expecting."

He wasn't wrong, but I hadn't even thought about that. I'd just thought maybe I was coming down with a bug. Johnny walked up and handed Connor the purple flip-flops I kept by the back door. Connor slipped them onto my feet, then closed the door. I couldn't hear what he said, but Johnny nodded his head and walked off in the direction of the clubhouse. When Connor got into the car, he started it up and headed for the main gate.

I didn't know who Doctor Myron was, but if Ridley was seeing him, maybe he was nice. Venom didn't seem like the type to let his woman go to a mean doctor. I didn't even know if Venom and Ridley were married, or if he'd just claimed her the way Connor had claimed me. Part of me wished there was a ring on my finger. I didn't know if that would ever happen, though. Connor took good care of me, and he was sweet to me, but he didn't love me. I didn't know that he would ever love me. Unfortunately for me, I was pretty sure I was already in love with the man.

At the doctor's office, Connor carried me inside, then made me sit while he checked me in at the counter. He returned with a clipboard, and I filled out the new patient forms. My dad had always made sure I had health insurance, but I didn't know if it would cover having a baby. I added the information to the sheet just in case. I signed my name across the bottom, and Connor dropped the forms at the front desk. A few minutes later, my name was called, and Connor carried me up to the counter. I felt ridiculous. My foot hurt, but I was almost certain I could walk on it. He eased me down onto my feet, and I tried not to glare at him over my shoulder.

"Miss VanHorne, your insurance requires a twenty-five dollar co-pay," the woman in pink scrubs said.

I felt Connor at my back, and he handed the lady a credit card. She swiped it, had him sign the receipt. He tried to pick me up again, but I pushed at him, determined to walk. It hurt a little, but it was manageable. We sat and waited again. The minutes ticked by and it felt like we'd been waiting forever. By the time they called my name, my ass hurt from sitting for so long. They weighed me, took my temperature, and checked my blood pressure. The nurse didn't say much as she recorded the information, but I noticed her eyes seldom left Connor. She was practically eating him up with her gaze. Heifer even licked her lips as she scanned him from head to toe. If I had to guess, I'd put her somewhere in her thirties, which meant she should have known better than to eye Connor like that, especially with me sitting right here. When she was finished eye-fucking my man and taking my vitals, she escorted us to a room and handed me a gown.

"You'll need to strip down and put that on. Your dad can wait in the hall," the nurse said, casting Connor a flirtatious smile.

Connor growled and narrowed his eyes. "She's not my fucking daughter."

The nurse pursed her lips, and a look of disgust crossed her face before she backed out of the room. I'd known not everyone would accept our relationship, but experiencing it firsthand didn't feel so great. I took off my clothes and pulled on the gown before sitting on the table. The paper crinkled under my ass. Connor had taken up residence across the room, leaned back against the wall with his arms folded and his ankles crossed. He looked fucking pissed too. Great.

Thanks a lot, nurse bitch! If I was pregnant and that woman had ruined this visit, I was going to scream. I didn't want Connor to look back on the day he found out he'd be a daddy and remember that woman's words. I fully intended to say something to the doctor. Obviously, the woman didn't know how to be a professional.

A man came in and smiled at us, holding out his hand to me. "You must be Isabella. I'm Dr. Myron."

I shook his hand, surprised that he looked so young. He couldn't be more than twenty-five. I glanced at Connor, and his eyes were narrowed again. Something told me Ridley had left out the part where her doctor was young and good-looking. Venom didn't seem like the type to tolerate another man looking at his wife's lady bits, and I didn't think Connor was going to appreciate it either. Not that I was married to Connor, but I was his just the same.

Dr. Myron turned toward Connor and held out his hand. "And you're the possible father-to-be?"

Connor nodded and shook the man's hand.

"Your nurse is rude," I said.

Connor's head jerked my way, and the doctor gave me a perplexed look.

"Which nurse?" Dr. Myron asked.

"The blonde who checked my weight and stuff, then brought me to this room."

"Cindy was rude to you?" he asked, still looking confused.

"Not me, exactly, but she kept looking at Connor like she wanted to lick him from head to toe. Then when she found out he's not my dad and that we're together, she looked disgusted and ran off."

Connor scowled at me, and I realized I'd used his real name in public. I'd forgotten that outside the house I was supposed to call him Torch. It had just slipped out.

Dr. Myron's eyebrows rose, and he stepped into the hall.

While he was gone, Connor glared me.

"I didn't mean it," I said. "I'm just so used to calling you Connor at home that I didn't even think about it."

He sighed and cracked his neck. "It's fine, baby. Just try not to do that at the clubhouse."

The doctor returned with nurse bitch in tow.

"Cindy, did you insult my patient and her husband?" Dr. Myron asked.

Cindy's jaw tightened. "She's just a kid. It's perverted."

"Since I know you saw Isabella's file, you're well aware that she's an adult. It's not your place to judge our patients. You owe Isabella and her husband an apology," Dr. Myron said.

I bit my lip so I wouldn't correct him. That's twice he'd called Connor my husband. I glanced his way, but he didn't seem bothered by the word. Cindy looked like she'd been sucking on raw lemons, but she spat out an apology and left. Dr. Myron didn't look pleased as he shut the door and turned to face us again.

"She's on probation. Or she was. I can assure you that once this appointment is over, she will no longer be in my employ. I'm very sorry for her behavior," Dr. Myron said. "Now, let's start with some basics. I see on your forms that your last period was six weeks ago."

"Yes," I said.

"And that's why you think you're pregnant?" Dr. Myron asked.

"She was throwing up this morning," Connor said.

Dr. Myron nodded.

"My, um... my breasts have been more tender than usual. I just thought maybe my period was about to start. They always get tender when it's that time of the month."

"Well, the first thing we need to do is a pregnancy test. I'm going to have someone come and draw some blood. I prefer using that over urine because the results are more accurate, especially this early. I'll send Tricia in, and once we have the results, I'll come talk to you."

"How long do the results take?" Connor asked.

"Not long. As long as the lab isn't backed up, we should have an answer in about fifteen minutes. We handle everything in-house, so I don't have to send it out somewhere."

Connor nodded, and Dr. Myron walked out, closing the door behind him.

"I know you were busy this morning. You didn't have to come with me," I said softly, looking down at my lap. "I'm sure Johnny would have brought me, or one of the other Prospects."

"Do you not want me here?" he asked.

My gaze jerked up to his. "Of course I want you here. I wanted to wake up beside you! But I know that can't happen all the time. I know that you have things to do, a club to run. I'm just trying not to be a burden to you."

His gaze hardened, and he came forward, his hand gripping my hair and tilting my head back. "Let's get one thing straight right now, baby. You are not now, nor have you ever been a burden to me. You're my woman. Mine. I will always be there for you. Is the shit going on at the club important? Yes. Is it more important than you? No."

His touch softened, and he kissed me, his lips lingering a moment.

A nurse bustled into the room, smiling brightly at us. "Ready for me to stick you?"

I hated needles, so not especially, but I held out an arm for her. Connor held my hand while the nurse got the blood she needed, then said the doctor would return with the results shortly. Once the door was closed, Connor's lips were on mine again. His tongue thrust into my mouth as his hands landed on my waist. My legs spread, and he stepped between them.

"Knowing you're naked under this scrap of fabric is making me hard as fuck," he murmured against my lips. He gripped the gown and started to lift it, but I reached out placed my hands on his wrists.

"Connor, someone could come in."

He growled softly, kissed me harder, then took a step back. Passion was blazing in his eyes, and I knew I'd come really close to being fucked in the doctor's office. As it was, there was now a wet spot under me because he had me dripping. If the doctor had to look at me down there, I was going to die of mortification. Connor went back to his position against the wall, but there was no hiding the fact he was hard. His jeans were molded over the hard ridge. He noticed my gaze on his crotch and reached down to adjust himself.

"If you don't stop looking at me like that, I'm going to lock that damn door and fuck you. I don't give a shit who hears your screams."

My eyes widened a moment, and I looked away. I had no doubt that he was dead serious. As much as I wanted to feel him inside me, this wasn't the time or place. There was no way I was going to spend the rest of my appointment with cum dripping out of me. I glanced at Connor, and he was smirking at me. The ass. He knew what he was doing to me and was enjoying every minute.

The doctor returned a short while later, and for that I was thankful. If I'd been left alone in this room with Connor for much longer, I might have actually let him take me on this padded table. My body pulsed with need, and I swear it felt like my clit had its own heartbeat. Dr. Myron looked from me to Connor. He grinned a little when he saw Connor's state, then faced me again.

"Well, congratulations." Dr. Myron smiled. "You're pregnant. We can try an ultrasound if you'd like, see if we can hear the baby's heartbeat. If you're six weeks, we should be able to. Any earlier than that, and we'd need a vaginal ultrasound."

"Uh." I looked at Connor who stared at the doctor like he'd grown a second head. I looked back over at Dr. Myron. "If I'm pregnant, I'm less than a month right now. I wasn't with anyone before that. So, I guess that means the regular ultrasound wouldn't work."

"What the fuck is a vaginal ultrasound?" Connor asked.

"Instead of using a smaller wand over her stomach, we'd use a longer one that has to go inside her. It's inserted vaginally." Dr. Myron smiled a little. "A little like a sex toy, but it's attached to a machine that will let you see and hear your baby."

Connor was shaking his head before the doctor even finished.

Dr. Myron seemed amused. "Would it make any difference if I told you I was in a committed relationship, and that my boyfriend is more than enough for me?"

"Boyfriend?" I asked.

Dr. Myron winked at me. "I have a thing for older men too."

I giggled and finally understood why it didn't bother Venom for Ridley to come see Dr. Myron. The man wasn't the least bit interested in her lady parts, or any lady parts for that matter. I'd be willing to bet he'd enjoyed that glance at Connor's hard cock, though. The look on Connor's face said he still didn't like the idea of the vaginal ultrasound, and considering how wet I was right now, I really didn't want one either.

"We can wait and try an ultrasound at your next appointment. I want you to come back in four weeks. We can get a better idea of a possible due date by then. I don't want to do anything that will make either of you uncomfortable, unless it can't be helped." Dr. Myron looked at Connor. "You're not going to castrate me when I have to deliver the baby, are you? Looking at certain parts of her will be inevitable."

"Fuck," Connor muttered.

I didn't know what the silly man thought would happen. If he hadn't wanted another man to look between my legs, he should have found a female doctor for me.

Dr. Myron focused on me again. "I'm going to call in a prescription for prenatal vitamins for you. You can start them tomorrow. Most of my patients prefer taking them with their breakfast. If the nausea gets too bad, I can give you something for that too."

"I was still a little nauseated after I threw up, but I've been fine since we've been here," I said.

"Good. Maybe you'll only have it in the mornings, then. Some women have morning sickness all day for the first trimester, and a rare percentage have it almost the entire pregnancy."

I wondered if I looked as horrified as I felt.

"The ladies up front will get your next appointment set up. If you need to reschedule, be sure to call twenty-four hours in advance or there's a cancellation fee of fifty dollars." Dr. Myron shook my hand, then Connor's. "I'll see you in a month."

He left, and Connor helped me get dressed, then we walked up front and set up my next appointment. I still felt a little dazed. Connor wasn't showing much emotion, and it worried me. We'd talked about the possibility of kids, and he'd seemed to want them. Had he changed his mind? He hadn't so much as cracked a smile when the doctor had confirmed the pregnancy. Did he not want this baby?

The ride back to the compound was quiet. I stared out the window, not knowing what to say, or if I should say anything at all. I didn't like the way I was feeling right now. My hand went to my belly. No matter what Connor thought about this pregnancy, I already loved the child growing inside me. The moment the doctor had said I was pregnant, I knew I wanted this baby. I just didn't know what would happen if Connor decided he didn't.

I was fighting back tears as we reached the house. Connor shut off the truck and unlocked the house. He stayed on the porch, standing in the doorway.

"I'll be back in a little while," he said. "Have a few errands to run."

"Fine," I said softly, refusing to cry in front of him.

He stared at me a moment, then shut the door and left. I heard the rumble of his motorcycle, and then I was alone. *No. Not alone.* I rubbed my belly. I'd never be alone again. Even if Connor decided he didn't want us, I'd always have a part of him.

"Why did you make me love you?" I asked, staring at the door where he'd stood moments before.

Sighing, I turned and went upstairs. All I wanted to do was sleep. Maybe after a nap things would look better.

Chapter Eight

Torch

Pregnant. Isabella was pregnant.

Even with my suspicions, and hearing the confirmation from the doctor, I still couldn't quite wrap my head around it. At fifty-one, I'd thought I'd never have kids. It was good to know my swimmers worked, apparently really damn well. I should have asked more questions at the appointment, but I hadn't been thinking clearly. I was so amped up, my cock aching for Isabella, that I'd just wanted the hell out of there. Then on the way home, I'd realized what I needed to do.

She'd been mine for three years. My name was inked on her skin, a warning to any who came near her that she was already claimed. But as I thought about raising a family with her, I knew that wasn't enough. Dr. Myron had called me her husband several times during the visit, and fuck if that didn't sound damn nice. I'd never wanted to get married. Isabella was already mine, and by the club's standards, she was my wife. But I wanted the rest of the world to see her that way too. I wanted her to share more than my home. I wanted her to share my name.

After I picked up her prenatal vitamins, I stopped by the jewelry store on Main Street. I idled my bike at the curb and put a call in to Wire. If anyone could fix this, it would be him. The man could make anything happen if it could be done through a computer.

"Yeah, Pres. What do you need?" Wire asked.

"I need a marriage license. I want to marry Isabella, and I want to do it tonight. I don't give a shit what you have to do, make it happen."

"Uh. You're getting married?"

"Yes, dipshit. Just do as I say. I need that piece of paper by tonight. If you can't make it happen through that computer of yours, do whatever you have to. I don't care who you have to threaten, fuck, or pay off."

"You got it," Wire said.

I disconnected the call and stepped into the small shop. The woman behind the counter didn't look very impressed with me. Her disdain was clear even from across the room. I browsed the cases until I found the selection of wedding rings. Maybe I should have asked her to marry me first, given her an engagement ring, but I didn't want to wait.

A platinum set caught my attention. The man's ring was just a plain band, but the woman's had small diamonds scattered around it. It wasn't overly flashy. It was delicate, like my woman, and I knew Isabella would love it. I pointed to the set.

"I want those."

The woman came and looked down into the case. She stared down her nose at me. "That set is three thousand dollars."

I pulled out my wallet and took out my bank card. "You accept Visa?"

The woman took the card from me, careful not to touch my fingers. She ran it through her machine, and when it cleared, which I'd known it would, she pulled the rings out of the case. I slid the man's ring onto my finger and was glad to see it was the right size. I only hoped Isabella's would fit her too. The snooty woman put the rings into boxes, then handed them to me. I shoved them into my pocket and walked out. Wasn't the first time someone had treated me like trash, and I knew it wouldn't be the last. But if anyone ever thought to do that to my son or daughter, I'd beat the shit out of them.

If I weren't on my bike, I'd have picked up some flowers for Isabella. The woman deserved the moon, and I'd give it to her if I could. I felt my phone vibrate, and I pulled it out at a stoplight.

Wire: It's done.

Me: Call Preacher. See if he's still ordained. I want this done at seven tonight.

Wire: Where did you plan on doing this?

Me: Clubhouse. No club sluts allowed in the compound tonight.

Wire. Consider it done.

I went straight home, hoping like hell Isabella had a dress that would work for tonight. Maybe I should have given her a proper wedding, with flowers and shit, but I wasn't a very patient man. Now that the idea had settled in my head to make her my official wife, I wanted it done. And I wanted it done now.

The lights were off in the house, and when I stepped inside it was eerily quiet.

"Isabella," I called out.

I didn't hear anything. I searched for her room by room, finally locating her in our bedroom. She was curled in the middle of the bed, but the tearstains on her cheeks gutted me. I stretched out next to her and smoothed her hair back from her face. Her breathing was deep and even, and it was obvious she'd cried herself to sleep. I was such an asshole. I hadn't meant to be, but it didn't change anything. In my determination to get married right-fucking-now, I'd hurt her.

"Bella," I said softly. "Wake up, baby. We need to talk."

Her eyes fluttered open. A flash of happiness lit up her face when she saw me, then she shuttered her expression.

"I'm sorry I took off like that, but I had something I needed to take care of," I told her. "There's something we need to do tonight. I need you to get up and shower, then put on a pretty dress."

"We're going out?" she asked, pushing up on an elbow.

"Not exactly, but you'll want to look your best." My fingers trailed over her cheek. "Although, I've never seen you look less than stunning."

She snorted. "I'm a mess."

"You're my mess, and you're beautiful. I'm sorry if I hurt you and made you cry. I didn't mean to."

"When you didn't say anything on the way home and then just left, I thought maybe you were upset about the baby. I thought..." She bit her lip. "I thought maybe you didn't want it, or me."

I pulled her against my chest. "I want you. I want both of you. Christ, haven't you figured it out, Bella? I love you so fucking much it hurts."

Her breath hitched. "You love me?"

"Yeah, baby. I love you."

She started crying again, and I didn't know what I'd done wrong this time.

"I l-love you t-too."

"Go get ready, baby. I'll shower in the guest bathroom. If I get in there with you right now, I'll want to fuck you, and then we'll be late."

I kissed her, then rolled out of bed before I was tempted to do more. She scurried into the bathroom, and I pulled out my best pair of jeans, a black button-down shirt, and some clean socks and underwear, then headed down the hall toward the other bathroom. I showered and dressed, then returned to the bedroom. Isabella was standing in front of the bathroom mirror, blowing her hair dry in the sexiest damn bra and panties I'd ever seen. I leaned against the bathroom doorway and just admired her.

After she'd dried and brushed her hair, she pulled it up in some sort of fancy knot, then put on a little makeup. I personally thought she was gorgeous without the crap she'd put on her face, but I knew women thought it made them prettier.

"I'm going downstairs to wait on you. If I stay up here, I might not be able to control myself." I winked at her, then went down the kitchen to wait.

Getting married in my motorcycle boots and cut probably wasn't something Isabella would approve of, but I was the damn club president. If I'd rented a tux and monkey shoes, the guys would have laughed me out of the damn clubhouse. When I heard her heels clicking across the floor, I turned and my breath froze in my lungs. She'd put on a cream-colored dress that hugged her curves like a second skin. It was made of some sort of lacy stuff, and fuck if I'd ever seen a more beautiful woman.

"You ready, baby?" I asked, my voice more gravelly than usual.

She smiled and nodded.

We took the SUV over to the clubhouse, and when we got out, she gave me a curious look. The parking lot was packed, and it looked like everyone was here. Well, most everyone. I knew Rocky was still off on his mountain top, beating himself up over something that had been out of his control. Maybe one day soon he'd return to us. I opened the door and ushered her inside, but she froze just over the threshold.

I looked over the top of her head and smiled when I saw the room had been decorated with what looked like white Christmas lights. Someone had strung them around the room by the ceiling. The tables had been pushed back a little to give us more room, and the assholes had even found an arch somewhere. Preacher was standing under it waiting on us, and the rest of the club was packed into the area near the bar. The few old ladies we had were present as well, even though none of them had bothered to get to know Isabella yet. I'd be speaking to their men about that shit. Either those women fell in line, or they weren't welcome here.

"Connor," she said softly. "What's going on?"

"You'll see, baby. Come on."

I took her hand and led her over to where Preacher stood. I reached into my pocket and pulled out the ring boxes, handing them over to Venom. He came up beside me, and Ridley stood on the other side of Isabella. My poor woman looked so damn confused.

Ridley was trying not to laugh. "You haven't figured it out yet, have you?"

Isabella shook her head.

"You're getting married!" Ridley squealed and bounced on her toes.

"Woman, stop bouncing before you knock my kid out there," Venom said.

She narrowed her eyes at him, but stopped bouncing up and down.

"Married?" Isabella asked, looking up at him. "You want to marry me?"

"I kind of liked Dr. Myron calling me your husband. Figured we'd make it official. You're mine in every other way that counts. Might as well make you mine on paper too."

A smile spread across her lips, and she threw her arms around me, hugging me tight.

Preacher cleared his throat. "Are the two of you ready?"

Isabella nodded, and she placed her hands in mine. I didn't hear half of what came out of Preacher's mouth; my gaze was fastened on my beautiful bride. There was such joy in her eyes, and a rosy glow to her cheeks. Venom cleared his throat behind me and jolted me back to the present.

I took the rings from him, and Isabella and I exchanged vows. When Preacher said I could kiss my bride, I pulled Isabella in close, her body pressed against mine, and I kissed her deeply. Catcalls and whistles rang out around the room as my wife melted against me. I knew this was our night, and everyone was expecting a party, but they would likely be partying without us.

Venom handed a glass of juice to Isabella and another to Ridley, while a Prospect handed out beers to everyone else. We stayed and mingled for a short while, then I led Isabella back out to the SUV, sneaking out while no one was paying attention. I helped her up onto the passenger seat, then pressed my lips to hers. She moaned and leaned closer to me. If she kept that shit up, I'd be fucking her in the damn parking lot.

"Home," I mumbled against her lips. "We're going home. Then I'm going to fuck you."

She shivered in anticipation, and I practically ran around to the other side of the truck, getting in and spitting gravel as I tore out of the lot and toward home. When we pulled in, Isabella nearly dove out of the truck and ran up the steps. I swatted her ass as I unlocked the door. She stepped into the front entry, and the door had barely shut before she was on me.

Her fingers were working the buttons on my shirt while her lips fused to mine.

If I'd known marrying her would make her this hot, I'd have done it a lot sooner. Fuck! It was like she was on fire. She pushed my cut and shirt off my shoulders, then started on my pants. She jerked at my belt until it came undone, then quickly unfastened my jeans. Her tongue thrust into my mouth as she worked my jeans and boxer briefs down my hips until my cock sprang out, hard and ready for her.

Her hand was so damn small, she couldn't even wrap it all the way around my dick, but I thrust against her palm, loving the feel of her hands on me. I reached for her dress, slowly pulling it up to her waist. As sexy as the panties were, they had to go. I tore them from her body, and she gasped, looking up at me, dazed.

"I'll buy you new ones," I said, turning to press her back to the door.

I stroked her pussy with my fingers and groaned at how fucking wet she was. I fucked her with one finger, then two, then three. She was panting and begging for more when I lifted her legs around my waist and thrust my cock deep inside her. Isabella cried out, her head going back and her eyes closing. Pure pleasure was etched on her face as she took all of me. I slammed into her, again and again, each thrust harder than the last. The door rattled in the frame as I pounded her sweet pussy.

Isabella came, coating me with her cream, as she cried out my name. I stilled inside her, wanting to hold off my orgasm. She felt too fucking incredible for this to end so soon. I pulled out and carried her upstairs, where I stripped the rest of our clothes from our bodies.

"Hands and knees at the side of the bed, baby," I commanded.

She shuddered and did as I said. I ran a hand down her rounded ass before pushing her legs farther apart. It spread her pussy open and gave me a glimpse of that other tight hole I'd like to fuck. I leaned forward and bit her ass cheek, making her yelp and look at me in surprise over her shoulder.

I coated my fingers again, thrusting them in and out of her, before I lined my cock up with her pussy and entered her hard and fast. I pushed her head down toward the bed, knowing it would let me take her deeper. With the new angle, my cock slid in farther. My strokes were slow and steady, building her up again. I toyed with her ass, her cream letting my finger slide inside. She moaned and thrust back against me.

"You like that, baby? You like it when I play with your ass?"

"Yes!"

My finger went in deeper, and soon I was fucking her ass with two fingers.

"What do you want, Bella?"

"I want you to fuck me."

I chuckled and thrust my cock and fingers into her again. "I thought I was."

"I want more," she begged.

"More what? You want another finger in your ass? Stretching you wide?"

She whimpered. I continued to work her and did add a third finger. Her body was trembling, and I could tell she was close to coming. Her pussy was so fucking hot, and she was so damn wet. I watched as my cock slid out, then back in, shiny from her cream.

"Harder. Please, Connor. I need it."

I thrust harder, my fingers and cock keeping time. I worked her good, making her entire body flush. My balls drew up, and I knew I was seconds away from coming. I moved my hand from her hip around her belly, and down between her legs. I groaned when I felt my cock sliding in and out of her, then started circling her clit. It didn't take much before she was screaming my name, thrusting back, fucking herself on my cock.

When she quieted, and I knew she was spent, I eased my fingers out of her ass and gripped her hips with both hands, taking her hard, fast, and deep. My cum shot out of my cock and filled her up, jet after jet bathing her insides as I fucked it into her. I didn't stop thrusting, even after the last drop of cum was wrung from me. Somehow, I was still fucking hard.

"Still feel good, baby?" I asked, fucking with her slow strokes.

"So good," she mumbled.

I pulled out and flipped her over. Grabbing her feet, I placed them on the mattress so that her legs were bent and spread wide. I dragged her ass to the edge of the mattress and then thrust into her again. Her gaze was fastened on mine as I took her again. But this time wasn't as fierce. I took my time, wringing every drop of pleasure from her I could, and only when I knew she couldn't handle any more did I finally let myself come again.

"Love you," she murmured, half asleep.

I picked her up and tucked her under the covers, then cleaned up in the bathroom before sliding in next to her. Pulling her against my chest, I kissed the top of her head. "Love you too, Bella."

She smiled and snuggled closer. I watched her, taking in her beauty, and marveling at the fact that I'd actually gotten fucking married. And I couldn't have been happier. With Isabella in my arms, and a baby on the way, my life was pretty fucking perfect. She might have made me wait three damn years, but the past month with her had been worth every second, and we had the rest of our lives to make up for lost time.

I traced the shell of her ear with my nose, then whispered, "Mine."

A smile curved her lips, and I knew that was a sight I'd never get tired of. I vowed right then, whatever it took, I'd make sure I saw that smile every day for the rest of our lives. She was my greatest gift, the most precious thing in the world to me, and I'd make sure she knew it. The fact she'd doubted me earlier, had thought I didn't want her or the baby, made my stomach sour. I knew I'd make her cry again, at some point. But I also promised that she'd never cry herself to sleep again.

She was mine. My everything. My fucking heart and soul.

And I was never letting her go.

Harley Wylde

Short. Erotic. Sweet.

Harley's other half would probably say those words describe her, but they also describe her books. When Harley is writing, her motto is the hotter the better. Off the charts sex, commanding men, and the women who can't deny them. If you want men who talk dirty, are sexy as hell, and take what they want, then you've come to the right place.

Harley Wylde is the "wilder" side of award-winning author Jessica Coulter Smith. Visit Jessica's website at jessicacoultersmith.com/ or Harley's website at harleywylde.com/. Join her Facebook fan group, Harley's Wyldlings, for book discussions, teasers, and more. For fans of Gay Romance, Harley/Jessica also writes as Dulce Dennison.

Find more books by Harley Wylde at changelingpress.com/harley-wylde-a-196.

Changeling Press E-Books

More Sci-Fi, Fantasy, Paranormal, and BDSM adventures available in E-Book format for immediate download at ChangelingPress.com -- Werewolves, Vampires, Dragons, Shapeshifters and more -- Erotic Tales from the edge of your imagination.

What are E-Books?

E-Books, or Electronic Books, are books designed to be read in digital format -- on your desktop or laptop computer, notebook, tablet, Smart Phone, or any electronic ebook reader.

Where can I get Changeling Press e-Books?

Changeling Press ebooks are available at ChangelingPress.com, Amazon, Barnes and Nobel, Kobo, and iTunes.

Changeling Press, LLC

ChangelingPress.com

CPSIA information can be obtained
at www.ICGtesting.com
Printed in the USA
LVHW111459090420
652806LV00001BA/61